# Minecraft Journey of Fear

# Chapter 1

Steve Persson was about to go on one of his first plane rides. He was, in fact, 41 years old, so that means he hasn't really had a lot.

He started packing his things. He packed a book, some leather clothes, and a laptop. He thought that was all he needed, after all, he wasn't going to a 3rd world country; he was only going to Scotland from south England.

Steve was going to visit his 1st cousin, whose name was Markus. Markus always had been in his 'own little land'. Steve waved this off as nonsense by a crazy man. Markus never visited Steve, and vice versa.

"I hope you'll be safe!" said his grandmother. She was 113 years old, now as the longest living person in all of Britain.

"Yes, grandma! Don't worry! If anything goes wrong, I will have a parachute to save me." Replied Steve, getting just the slightest bit bugged by her incessant warning.

Steve closed his suitcase abruptly. He hugged his grandmother and was off.

He lived quite inconveniently near an airport, so he always heard the roaring of planes going over his house. But now, that is a good thing, because he just has to cross a street, and walk down a path for about 5 minutes until he gets there.

When he got there, he searched for a person to contact. He found one of his friends working there. He went over to talk to him

"Hi, I need to board a plane." Said Steve.

"Yeah, sure. I need to scan you though, for legal purposes. Take out anything metallic that you might think would trigger it, like, say, loose change, glasses, that sort of thing."

Steve did as instructed. He took out his laptop, his iron bookmark, and his wallet. Joe escorted him through the metal detector. No warning or big flashing lights appeared, so Steve relaxed.

"Yep, you're fine. Go on." Said Joe.

Steve walked onto the airplane. He was told to sit at seat 37, so he searched for it. 17, 18, 19, "Nope" thought Steve. "It's not around here." He moved on a bit and found number 34, 35, 36, 37!

"Ok! This is my seat, apparently. Isn't great, but isn't terrible."

Steve quickly took back the statement 'It isn't terrible' when he realised who were behind and in front of him.

Behind him, he had a bunch of noisy guys who were shouting every possible word that came into their head. And in front, was a terribly plane-sick person who threw up every 10 minutes or so. He really did feel like he was in the deepest possible pits of hell.

He decided there was no use being troubled about what he couldn't stop, so he laid down his head on a pillow that used to be on his seat, but now was on the side of the wall, being held there by the weight of his own head.

Eventually, he drifted off to sleep.

# Chapter 2

He woke up suddenly. He looked up and there was a warning light flashing and a voice blaring over the loudspeaker saying

"PUT YOUR TRADE TABLE UP AND SEAT BACK IN THE FULL ABROAD POSITION"

He did as he was told. Steve could feel the pressure increase as they went down. His ears burned with pain. He tried swallowing, but it didn't work well enough. He closed his eyes, and braced for impact.

He felt the blood drain out of his head, and he passed out.

He woke up. He looked around. He could see the plane burning, but no bodies. He wondered why for a moment, but his train of thought was interrupted by a creak of bending steel.

He wrenched a bit of steel off of himself, and then climbed out the window. He looked at what he could see. One thing he noticed immediately was that everything was cubic.

The trees, made of many blocks, the sand under his feet, made of many blocks. Even his feet and body were blocky. His head was a cube, his body and limbs cuboids.

He was slightly scared at sight of this unreal world.

To try something, he punched the sand he stood on. (It was the only thing he could do with his arms). The sand disappeared, and left a perfectly cubic hole in the ground. He walked into it. The sand went into his backpack.

He opened his backpack to get it out, because otherwise it would destroy his laptop and clothes, and book and what not, but when he opened it, the backpack filled his vision. And the backpack didn't even look ordinary, it had slots! And his laptop turned into something that looked like an iron ingot, and next to it, there was some red, dust sort of thing. He then closed his backpack.

He just stood there thinking for a while, and then decided he has to do something. He has to at least try to survive here. He thought "What is the most valuable thing I need right now?"

"Wood" he spoke out loud.

He looked around to find a nice looking tree, and found one. He walked towards it, and started punching it.

"This is me" he thought. "I am that guy on the beach, punching a tree that isn't even falling down."

He punched the wood out of quite a few trees, and then went on to build a house. It was small, with little lighting, but he suspected that it would do.

Outside, the sun was coming down, but the moon was coming up. He heard a growl.

"Get away! You stupid wolves!" he shouted as he banged the side of his house. The wolf took no notice. Instead, it gargled.

"I said, GET AWA- wait, did you gargle?" Steve now had a slight trace of fear in his voice. It punched the side of his house to reveal its face.

It had a green face, with sleeping eyes, and a foul, spit drooling mouth. It had half-broken teeth, and a blue shirt and trousers on.

Steve screamed and threw a handful of dirt at it, but the dirt had no effect. It still came through the wall. Steve punched it with as much force as he could possibly apply, but it kept coming, and it punched him. He fell back onto the ground, because of the extreme strength of the creature. Steve punched it in the mouth, but cut himself in the process. In one final fit of energy, he delivered a thankfully fatal blow to the lower jaw. The creature fell backwards and died.

"I don't like this place." Murmured Steve, with a trembling voice.

Steve fixed the breach on the wall, and lay down on the cold sand.

# Chapter 3

"What do you mean, we don't have any info on him?" shouted King Ender. He was very temperamental about what he wanted. "I am an Enderman! How DARE you not fulfil my orders! I SENTENCE YOU TO EXECUTION! Guards, take him away!"

On that exact note, two tall black figures got up from their hunched positions in the shadows, and grabbed the zombie and tore him apart. They took half each and ran over to the shadows to feast.

"Guards, open the creeper cages, stat!" shouted King Ender bitterly. The guards did what they were told immediately.

They drew a latch from the cage and 3 green things jumped out. They had a mouth that was curved downwards, and they looked sad as if they had to do something to someone they didn't want to. It had no arms, but four legs on the bottom of its body.

It immediately tried to escape out the door, but the guards blocked the path and held the creeper in place.

"Now send him to Steve! AT ONCE!" shouted King Ender angrily.

The guards grabbed the creeper quickly and teleported away in a fluster of purple smoke.

"Is there any other way to please you, sir?" asked a giant spider.

"Yes, actually. Make me some food. I want some mushroom and steak soup!"

"Yes, your highness." Replied the spider, with a bow of the head. It scuttled away into a small room with mushroom farms, wheat farms, melon farms, cow farms, pig farms, chickens farms, you name it, if it's to do with food, and it is in there.

Within a few moments, about 30 seconds of impatient demanding, the spider came out with mushroom and steak soup. He gave it to King Ender.

"Good. Now go back to your duties as Enderman forge. I NEED more." Snapped King Ender.

The spider scuttled into the forge room, filled with lava, water, and obsidian.

Suddenly, grey smoke got sucked into King Ender. He instantly knew what it meant.

"I want Steve DEAD. He killed one of my best soldiers. Not captured, not imprisoned, I WANT HIM DEAD!"

King Ender has a psychic connection with the other Endermen, so he was telling them that.

"Yes... sir... he... can't... take... much...more..." choked an Endermen. That Enderman was lucky enough to choke words, while many others could not make a sound. Only King Ender is allowed to speak properly.

"Well hurry up about it!"

"But... sir..."

"DON'T TALK BACK TO ME!"

"Yes… sir…"

"Is he going to die within the next 30 seconds, or not?"

"No… sir… he… is… too… strong…"

"AAARRRGGGHHH!!!" screamed King Ender as he smashed a wall. "I don't care… I WANT HIM DEAD!"

# Chapter 4

Steve woke up with a big surprise. He listened closely, he heard a monotonous hiss. He opened the door to have a look, and he was nose to nose with a large green animal. He jumped away.

"SssssorryssssSSSSSssss" said the creeper.

"Are you okay? Can you talk? You look sad! Hello? HELLO??" panicked Steve.

The creeper started crying out thick, dark smoke.

"SSSSsssssSSSSssssDIEssssSSSSssssNOWSsssssssSSS" said the creeper, struggling to get the words to his tongue.

"I didn't want to do this!" said Steve. He then opened his chest, and pulled out a wooden sword. He held it tightly, and charged into the creeper. First he saw the creepers eyes stop pouring out smoke, and then he felt the body go limp, and the creature evaporated into smoke. The smoke rose into the air and got sucked into one direction.

He saw two black figures sprint across the sky. He called them.

"Hey! You! Up there! Get down here! Did you send him?"

But they had already sprinted away.

Steve decided to stop looking for more, so he started looking underground. He went mining to try to calm himself down.

He found a sort of beige material, and when he touched it, he realized it was iron. He smelted and crafted it into an iron sword, and two iron shovels.

He decided he wasn't going to get anything done like this. He needed to kill every last monster from this island. This sudden urge of bloodlust was surprising to him, but it didn't put him off the idea.

He remembered Markus, and him being in his 'own little world'. He thought that maybe, just maybe, he lives here somewhere.

Steve knows that the only way he is going to get off here alive and if he wants to kill all of these enemies he has to find Markus. Markus told him that he was a skilled fighter, and that he needed it desperately in where he lives.

At once, he grabbed some of his stuff, cobblestone, tools, swords, iron, wood, and he set off. He walked outside, and it had become daytime again. He considered which way he should go first, so he stood still for a minute, and then started walking east.

# Chapter 5

"So you have failed me again?" asked King Ender angrily, so much so that you could almost see the rage boiling behind his long purple eyes.

"Greatest... apologies... sir..." coughed an Enderman. He was almost cowering before King Ender, because he had seen so many of his fellow Endermen get crushed before the mighty hand of King Ender. He didn't want to join them.

"Apologies? APOLOGIES? I do not accept your apologies! I will give you another chance, because you haves served me very well over the last few months, but one more slip up like that and..." King Ender snapped his fingers. After about 3 seconds of silence, he said "nothing will be left."

"I... shall... not... rest... until... he... is... dead..."

"If you can kill this Steve, then you will be greatly rewarded with a portion of land. If you kill him, you will be King Ender of your own land!! But not until he is here with his head at my feet. And remember, if you try anything, anything 'funny' then you shall be immediately killed, and recycled to feed your kin."

There was a slightly eerie pause.

"In fact, I'll send all my troops. Every spider, every zombie, every creeper and Enderman. And, if that doesn't work... let's just say I have a secret weapon." After that, King Ender laughed a bit.

"Sir... I... see... Steve... moving... he...is... going... somewhere... else..."

"Well chase him!"

"Yes... sir..."

The Enderman took off. He was flying at a considerable rate. He passed desert, and marsh, and jungle, and grasslands. But there was no sign of Steve. He looked and looked. He found Steve's old house, but it was abandoned and no one was in it. The Enderman flew down to see if he could salvage anything left behind. There was some flint and steel setup there, so he took that and burned down the house. And after that, he decided to burn more stuff. He burnt down a forest, grassland, a primitive village, and another wooden house.

Still no sign of Steve.

The Enderman was flying overhead when he found a movement in a cave. It flew close down to the cave and observed. Whoever –or whatever- was in there was not coming out for a while. The Enderman landed. It crept into the shadows and watched. There was a person in there, but was it Steve? The Enderman grabbed him from behind, but the person there wasn't Steve, he had no pupils. Only white eyes. This person punched the Enderman in the face from behind, teleported behind the Enderman, and ripped out his spinal column, then teleported away. The only thing left of the Enderman was a dead body, with an open back.

# Chapter 6

Steve had walked for a long time now, and he was getting hungry. He looked around for something to drink or eat, and he found a pig. He crept up to the pig and, when the pig wasn't looking and Steve was close enough, Steve jumped onto the pig and wrestled it to the ground. He took his sword and chopped off its head. He began the long process of getting the pork out of the pig, but when he finished, he realized something.

He was no longer bound as much by the laws of this cube land. His fingers had separated, and his eyes had a slight indent. He could also do other things with his arms than just punch things. He was quite pleased with this.

Steve quickly got distracted from moving his fingers when he saw a large fire come his way. It was spreading through both, grass and the trees around him. He took his pork and ran. The fire was spreading quickly. He had to hurry.

Finally he got away from the fire. He found a cave, although it was small, it would do. He saw a tall black figure land in front of it. He decided not to go in, but just watch. He saw it enter the cave, and then grab the guy in it. The person in it looked *just* like him, except he had empty eyes. No pupils, just white. The person there punched the black figure in the face, and appeared behind it, only to tear out the spinal column. In a heartbeat, the black figure was dead and the person was gone.

Steve stood there in amazement at this spectacle. He approached the dead black figure. It was most certainly dead. It had no spinal column, so it was almost certainly dead. Just to be sure, Steve poked it with a lengthy stick, but it was definitely dead.

He felt safer, but then more scared. He saw the person who could teleport and kill Endermen with two fatal blows. He was wondering if that person would return, and if they did, would it be for good or evil?

Steve tried to put these thoughts out of his mind by sifting through the chest across the dark room. Steve found some stuff that looked like blood-drenched cobblestone, and he found a glowing sort of glass stuff. He also found something that looked like very jagged obsidian. There was also a note. Steve picked it up and read:

'If you are reading this, then I have let my guard down, and you have not long to live. If you can live long enough to read this note, then I have the blueprints for what a hellgate looks like. They are enclosed underneath. If you see one, <u>DESTROY IT</u>. It will unleash terrors into this world that you could not imagine, screaming hordes of evil. I am going to have to absorb the energy of all hellgates near in order to close them in time. I am using a netherack - glowstone T-flip-flop gate to absorb it. I might be able to bypass it, or I will die. There is a small chance I will be a living host for the Nether, but there is one thing you must never do: don-sorry! It is starting…'

That was all the letter said. Underneath there was a picture with the blueprints of it, the hellgate. Steve was tempted to make a hellgate, but looked again at the note. He decided it was safer not to build one.

He lay down on the ground, but he realized the chest contained a bit of sheep wool. He took the wool, and used it as mattress and duvet. He went to sleep after a while of waiting.

# Chapter 7

Markus was locked up in a prison. He was chained to the wall by King Ender for being a port for the Nether to come through. Even King Ender wouldn't want that. That was one force even he didn't want to mess with. Markus could do nothing but think his earlier life. He still remembered how he first got there.

Going on an airplane trip to go to America to visit his family, but his airplanes wing was hit by a creeper, probably thrown by King Ender, and the plane crashed, and he landed on the island.

He sought shelter when he found a hellgate. It glowed, so brightly. He could hear screams and cries from it. He walked into it purely out of curiosity, but when he got in there, and he saw the tortured souls stuck in there, and fire, and lava coating everything, he changed his opinion. He wrote the letter and put it in his chest, and absorbed the Nether portal. He had forever since heard the screaming and tortured cries and moans of those who had died.

Markus had studied hellgates in what ever way he could, but he could not find much information about it anywhere. The only thing he could find were runes in ancient Notchen, about the hellgates being possessed by Herobrine, who was the devil of the land, and Notch, who was the god of the land.

But now he was trapped. In a cage, strapped to a wall. He could just reach a bucket of lava in his pocket. He dumped it out and poured a tiny amount on the chains. They weakened, so Markus knew he had to act fast, before the lava hardened into rock.

He pulled and pulled, and they finally broke. He was relieved. He remembered his fighting techniques and quickly acted out some of them to get into the flow of it.

He started walking towards the exit to get out of the place, but a zombie noticed him. Before the zombie could make a sound, Markus whipped round, drew his iron sword and cut off its head. As one act of sabotage, he opened the creeper gates for them to run free, and to blow up the stuff in their sabotage. He jogged out of the place, and before anyone noticed him, he was gone.

He was so relieved to finally be outside again. He did a little dance, and looked for the place where the remnants of the hellgate were, and where he left the note and blueprints.

He started a very long journey. Periodically, he would run into a creeper or a zombie, and very scarcely a skeleton.

Eventually he did find the cave. He walked inside and the first thing he saw was a dead Enderman on the floor, then he realised the remnants of the hellgate was gone, and lastly he found someone sleeping in a bed they had made!

"Oi! You! Get up! This is my bed!" shouted Markus, a bit annoyed.

Steve very slowly and carefully got up, and squinted at Markus.

"Yeah? Is it? Can I sleep here anyway?" asked Steve, who already was falling asleep again.

"I don't know! First actually get up. Don't just sit up and fall back to sleep."

There was no reply from Steve, so Markus grabbed Steve and pulled him off the bed.

"WAKE UP!" shouted Markus, who was really losing his patience now.

"FINE!" shouted Steve, as an imitation of Markus.

Steve stood up and looked at Markus.

"Who are you then?" asked Steve.

"I am Markus Persson."

"I am Steve Persson. Wait, did you say you are Markus? Do you have a cousin named Steve?"

"Yes. Are you that cousin?"

"I think so. Hi Markus! Now can I go back to sleep?"

"Fine…" sighed Markus.

# Chapter 8

King Ender was sitting down on a chair while 4 other Endermen carried him. He was in search of his escaped prisoner, Markus.

"Find him now! I don't want him running around without someone to keep him from building hellgates all over the area. We'll be lucky if he hasn't already made one. This is EXACTLY why I hired the skeletons to guard him. So that he doesn't run away! Guards! I want you to kill every skeleton within 100 mile radius! And spider! Hurry up with your Enderman forging! These Endermen aren't going to forge themselves you know!"

"Yes… sir…" choked an Enderman

"Yes sir." Said a spider.

The spider started doing it at a frantic speed, which was one Enderman every 10 seconds. Endermen are crafted out of obsidian and ender pearls. They have an automatic obsidian machine, and an Enderman drops an ender pearl every 2 minutes or so.

The Enderman jumped into the sky and flew around delivering fatal blows to many, many skeletons. He usually delivered the blow to the spine, or ribcage. Either way, the skeletons would die in a spray of bones that would litter the ground beneath it.

King Ender got out of his chair, and started flying instead.

"You are too slow for me! I would rather fly to my destination than have you snails carry me!" snapped King Ender. He raised his hand and the Endermen exploded. This put a wide grin on his face. After he finished watching the black shards dissipate, being broken into more and more shards and eventually becoming dust and blowing away, he wiped the grin off his face and flew to his destination.

It was a long journey. He, like the first Enderman in on the hunt, saw desert, forests, grassland, and the remnants of a marsh. A lot of it was blazing with fire.

He continued to search. He found the cave that the first one had seen. So, to check out all the nonsense revolving it, he landed to take a look. The first thing he saw was that there was a hellgate loose. That was also the only thing he saw because he flew away instantly on sight of that horrific thing.

He hid behind a rock to regain his breath. Could it really be a hellgate? Or was he just dreaming? King Ender realised the hellgate was real when he saw a large white jellyfish fly out of it.

"Ghast!" he gasped. "Endermen! GET HERE RIGHT AWAY! Code red! CODE RED! A Ghast from a hellgate!!"

"I... um... en... eet..." choked a less fortunate Enderman.

Within seconds, 30, give or take, Endermen had teleported in. The Ghast started shooting fireballs at them, and in about 10 seconds, half the army was dead. The Endermen started shooting the Ghast with a big gun. It was so big it needed a stand and 3 Endermen to operate it.

"Yes! Good plan, using a high powered glowstone concentrated laser beam magnified by an ender pearl! Or HPGCLBMBAEP. Yeah, a bit long. Who cares? It's killing the Ghast!"

With a few blows, the Ghast fell out of the sky and landed on the stand, which sent the HPGCLBMBAEP toppling down on top of the Ghast.

"Take the gunpowder from it! And also bring the whole thing, come to think of it. I bet everyone is hungry, besides. That thing is huge." Ordered King Ender.

King Ender didn't like what he saw, but it gave him an idea about what he is against.

# Chapter 9

Steve woke up sharply again. He was starting to get really tired of waking up sharply, so he didn't mind as much.

When he got up, at first he saw a person disappear at the very moment that he opened his eyes.

Then, when he got up to chase him, he saw that there was a hellgate next to him. He jumped when his bare skin pressed into the cold obsidian.

He remembered about what the note had told him. He instantly ran from the cave. He ran until he found Markus hiding in a tree. He was hunched over.

"Markus? Are you ok? You look a bit pale."

Markus said nothing, instead growled.

"Hello?"

Markus suddenly got up in a flurry of limbs, and broke through the branches and grabbed Steve. And raised his hand, and then brought it down swiftly on Steve's head.

Before he could do hit Steve, someone teleported behind him and grabbed Markus off of Steve and ripped off his head. The person teleported away immediately after.

The only thing Steve could see of the person is that he had a brown shirt on, and it was not ragged or showing any state of ware.

Back from the direction of his cave was a loud bang, that nearly deafened him, and almost ripped trees out of the very earth they were implanted in.

He heard a few blasts, and then he saw a large white jellyfish fall from the sky and make a loud crash, followed by an even louder crash. He started to continue his hasty journey away.

On the way, he killed a few pigs, chopped down a few trees, but what really interested him was the sight of a path. It was obviously man made, and made him wonder about where it leads to, so he followed it to its destination.

Steve could see in the distance a house. No, a few houses. No, a city of houses! It had tall buildings, short buildings, long buildings and narrow buildings, and plenty of houses that were for sale.

He walked up to the main gate and found a guard.

"Hello," he asked "Where exactly is this?"

"The city is named  Minsoon. It has a population of exactly 32 and is 2 kilometers long and 1 kilometer wide. It is open for business for building. If you wish to extend the city and make more houses and roads, then you are allowed in, if you wish to take up residence, the price is 25 gort. No more and no less. If you do not wish to take up residence or to build or work in any way whatsoever, the price is 5 diamonds to go in."

"Hmm, I think I will work here. I need the money. What did you say the currency is? Gort? How many gort do I get for every house I erect?"

"You get 25 gort for every house you erect. 1000 gort can buy a gold bar and 1 iron ingot."

"I see. I shall work here then. May I come in, guard?"

"Yes. We are always welcoming new workers or residents."

Steve walked inside the gates, and found that the place wasn't very populated. There was only 1 person out walking, so Steve went over to talk to him.

"Hello? Oh, hello! I'm new here; can you help me on what I should do? I just got here. I came here to work, where do I get the materials and where do I start building houses?"

"I see you have a lot of questions" replied the man. He was quite old, but didn't have an old voice. "First question, yes, I can help you on what to do, I am the town hall ruler, or mayor, and I work at keeping the place in regulation and making sure no body kills each other or starts a riot, and I also host the church to Notch."

"To Notch? Now, I also worship him, because he is the only god I know of. I know that there are other gods, but Notch is the only one I can think of. Anyway, where do I get the materials to build the houses?"

"Yes, I'll show you. Follow me, and in the mean time, I shall give you a tour."

Steve started following this person down a smooth road. It looked so smooth you could slide across it like ice, but when he touched it was quite coarse.

"Here is the bakery. In there, a lady named Granny Bacon lives in there. Her job was passed down from her family, you know. Her grandmother brought the shop – that means that she erected it, and she lived in it, and then she started selling the most delicious pastries and bread in all of Minecraftia! Care to come in and have a taste? They really are great."

"Yes, I suppose I am a bit hungry anyway."

They opened the door to the bakery, and found a nice place with tables, a menu, and cosy wallpaper.

"Hello, Granny Bacon!" said the mayor welcomingly.

"Hello, dear!" she replied.

"I was just showing… what was your name again?"

"Steve."

"Yes, that's it! Steve around town, and I thought that we could pop in to try one of your pastries, please."

"Certainly, boys. Do you want a custard tart? I made them freshly!"

"Mmm, sounds delicious. How much is that?" asked Steve as he dug into his pocket.

"Oh, nothing for you, dear. You haven't tried it yet, so I'll give you a free taster."

"Wow, thank you, Granny Bacon."

"Here you go, then! Eat up while it is still warm." Said Granny Bacon as she handed them both a custard tart. They were small, circular pastries with a sort of solidified custard in the centre.

Steve took a bite.

"Oh my god, this is delicious! You make great custard tarts! I'll be coming around later to get some more, definitely. Mmm, thank you so much, Granny Bacon!"

Steve ate his custard tart so quickly, by the time they had gone out the door, there was nothing left.

"So that is Granny Bacons bakery, and next to it, over here is the general vendor. The person who runs it is Alexei Strange. He sells stuff like eggs, milk, bread, wheat seeds, tools, wood, stone, etc. He does a good job as well. He goes out to get the milk and eggs himself, so you know it is good quality."

"Cool." Said Steve.

"And there is the butchers. The person in there is called Phil Diamond. He makes delicious meat, and seasons it just right. Legend has it, his father prepared food for Herobrine to drive him away. His father made 100 portions of steak, and gave it to Herobrine, and he has been busy eating it ever since. Maybe later you can have something from him."

"Sounds nice, I like steak and pork and stuff, so I will visit him frequently."

"And here we are, the supply store. Basically, really cheap prices on supplies. 64 pieces of wood for 1 gort. 32 pieces of stone for 1 gort. That is where you get your stuff from. You also get 2 gort for every 64 wood pieces you bring in. So, not a bad place to start off working for. The place is always stocked high because of the amount of new people we had joining us over the past few days."

"Well, I guess I should go and get some wood, then!"

And with that, Steve had set off in search of wood.

# Chapter 10

Markus was in a dark room. There was no exit, and no gravity. There was only darkness. However, he could see his own body and legs and what not.

"This must be what death feels like." He muttered to himself.

"Oh, yes. It most certainly is. You *are* dead." Said another voice, that seemed to come from every wall and corner of the room.

"Hello? Who are you? Where are you?" said Markus after he jumped because of the appearance of another voice from no where.

"I am Notch, the creator of all of Minecraftia! I have been disturbed from my regular watch over Minsoon, to escort you through the after life." Notch seemed to be Swedish, or somewhere in the vicinity of Sweden at least.

"You are Notch? I thought I would never live to see the day where I would find you!"

"Well, you didn't live to the day. You were possessed by a spirit of Herobrine and were forced to try to kill Steve, but I saved Steve. So now he isn't going to die."

"You aren't going to punish me for that, are you?" asked Markus with a slight quiver of fear in his voice.

"No, no. I shall grant you access to reincarnation. You are allowed to be reincarnated once, and then I shall have to keep you here. There is a person in Minstrool who recently died, would you like their body, Mark?"

"Yes, please, I don't really want to stay here for all of eternity, no offence to you Notch." Replied Markus, as he was sort of relieved not to be punished by Notch, and also not to be stuck in a plain black room for ever.

"Alright, then. I hereby reincarnate you as John!" said Notch as a bolt of lightning came down and struck Markus, causing at first pain, then sorrow, then happiness, and then pain again.

Markus sat up on a bed.

"Ooh, you don't look very well at all. Good thing I took you in. You were just laying there, in the middle of the path! Here, take this Propolis. It is said, that Notch himself makes Propolis and gives it to the bees and humans for good health! Really goes to show how much he loves us." Said a fairly old man, with a young voice. He just kept talking and talking, barely stopping to take a breath.

"Who are you?" Markus asked wearily.

"Me? I am the Mayor of Minstrool. I am also the priest at the holy church of Notch."

"My name is Markus."

Markus felt like there was something he had done, something he had seen, but couldn't quite put his finger on it.

"I come from… I come from… I don't know actually." Said Markus. His head felt very cloudy, but it felt like someone was dusting away the cobwebs in his brain.

"Well, maybe you just got dropped down from the sky by an Enderman, or another one of Herobrines minions. The best cure for evil is Propolis. I eat some of the stuff every day to cleanse my soul because in the church of Notch you aren't supposed to have any sins on your soul but I have heard that Propolis cleanses those sins right out and you don't have to be seen before Notch with sins on your soul so it's a good system." Said the mayor, Markus had to actually interrupt him to get him to stop talking.

"So, before you start talking again, sorry, no offence, but you do talk on a bit. Anyway, have you seen someone named Steve? I am a friend of his, I know it is a bit unlikely, I mean, through the whole world what are the odds that I would find him here, but, just tell me; is Steve here?"

"Steve? Is it? Yes, I took him on a tour a few days ago. Now I believe he is still gathering wood. He wanted a lot of gort. Well, who can blame him? We all want money! He's just more eager to do it then the rest of us. Good, though because we need some resources, especially wood, and he has earnt about 8 gort now. So that is what? 256 blocks of wood! Now that is quality lumber jacksonry. I know that isn't a real word, but it sounds so awesome. Do you-"

"Can I leave a note in the supplies shop for him? I need to find him."

"Yes, yes you can. I once left a note for someone at the supply shop, and they never came back. Although, that night I heard screams and growls, so he probably got eaten by wolves or something. That was sad, but we didn't have a funeral that night because King Ender was attacking, the nasty man. He pillaged almost the whole city, but we fought his minions off and are still rebuilding the houses. And we haven't finished it all but for some reason we are expanding the borders instead of fixing the broken bits! Talk about nonsense..."

"Well, can I borrow a bit of paper?" asked Markus impatiently.

"Yes, but I don't have any. Go see Granny Bacon in the bakery. She grows her own sugar and makes delicious pastry dishes. Out of the sugar cane she grows the can make paper, or sugar, or books. She gives a lot of the paper to the librarian who lives way down there and he makes it into books and sometimes sells them, but most of the time uses it as a library. So go see her and she might give you some sugar canes. To make paper."

"Okay, then. I am going now!" said Markus, who was trying to escape the chatter box to go and see Granny Bacon about it.

Markus finally did escape and walked into the bakery.

"Hello, dear!" said Granny Bacon welcomingly.

"Hello, Granny Bacon. Could I have a piece of paper from your sugar canes?"

"Yes. Gosh, I don't remember seeing you around town. Would you like a free taster custard tart? They don't seem to be selling so well for some reason."

"Yes, please."

Granny Bacon handed him a custard tart, and started walking to the back room with her sugar farm.

"I will be back soon! Just sit down and enjoy your custard tart."

Granny Bacon disappeared from sight and in about 3 seconds was back to the front with a sheet of nice, white paper.

"    ";

I have it. Come get your paper!"

"Thank you, Granny Bacon. Here, I will give you one of my diamonds!" said Markus gratefully as he put a fine cut diamond on the counter. After that, she put the paper down and admired her diamond.

"Thank you, dear-y!" called Granny Bacon, not taking her eyes off the diamond.

"You are most welcome." Said Markus.

Markus left the bakery and scribbled down a note on his paper. The note said:

To Steve:

Meet me at 17th Gorthen Avenue – my house

From Markus.

He posted that note on the supplies store, and then went to see a carpenter.

"Hello." Said Markus awkwardly.

"Hello." replied the carpenter. "What can I do for you?"

"Can you build me a house for…" Markus shuffled through his back pack. "4 diamonds? I need it to be on Gorthen Avenue, please."

"Hmm, yes. I can do that. How many floors?" asked the carpenter as he jotted down the order on a notepad as if he was a waiter.

"Only 2." Said Markus quite simply.

"Okely Dokely. Check back at 17 Gorthen Avenue tomorrow." Said the carpenter as he made his way to the supplies shop.

"Thank you!" called Markus as he threw the carpenter 4 diamonds.

"No problem." Said the carpenter.

Markus thought he probably should go and wait at 17 Gorthen Ave., so that Steve could find him, so Markus did go wait there. And he waited for a while.

# Chapter 11

King Ender was flying away very quickly from the Ghast corpse.

"Hurry up! That thing might get back up!" shouted King Ender, as he was ordering away his troops from the hellgate.

"Ess... sor..." choked most of the Endermen.

They flew very quickly back to the castle they had stayed at for a while. King Ender sat back down on his throne, and the Endermen got back into their cages.

"Now, I bet I know who made this hellgate." Said King Ender between breaths. "It was that wretched prisoner! Find out where he is, guards!"

"Eee... iss... in... mit...roon..."

"Minsoon?"

"Ess..."

"Then I shall burn their land down with my army. They may have won last time, but then we didn't have any Endermen because we couldn't forge them. But now... now we have over 100 Endermen! We will conquer their land!!"

"What about their weaponry? They still have the HPGCLBMBAEPs, don't they? They could kill 100 Endermen in one shot, if they did it right! The Ender Pearls gave us life, but used in the right way can also take life away from us!" said a skeleton very bravely.

"Do you honestly think my forces are feeble enough to get destroyed by a few shots of BRIGHT LIGHT!? I would not DARE go in to battle with a doubtful twerp like you!" shouted King Ender. King Ender raised his hand and the skeleton exploded. "Let that be a lesson to all of you. Have faith in me, and YOU WILL BE FINE!"

There was a fairly long silence, and then King Ender spoke again.

"Send in all the troops to Minsoon city. All the creepers, all the skeletons, all the zombies, all the Endermen, and all the spiders all to Minsoon city."

Suddenly the Endermen grabbed the creepers and kept their fuse from blowing, and the spiders carried the skeletons. The zombies were left to idle on by themselves.

The creepers and Endermen were in front, and then just behind were the spiders and skeletons. And obviously, last were the wave of millions of zombies.

"How many Endermen are there *exactly*?" asked the Ender King.

"There are 133 Endermen exactly." Replied the spider who was managing the troops and what not.

"How many creepers are there *exactly*?"

"There are 62 creepers."

"How many spiders? Not including you."

"There are 423 spiders."

"How many skeletons?"

"312 skeletons."

"And lastly, how many zombies are there?"

"4,747,400 zombies."

"Very good. Very good indeed."

# Chapter 12

Steve had chopped down many trees. He had made about 16 gort, and he was about to get 2 more gort.

He needed to drop off the wood he had chopped at t he supplies shop, so he went there and put it through a small chute that feeds through the wall. He heard a whirring noise, and then it dropped down 2 small coins in a chute next to it. He picked up the coins and stuffed them into his pocket.

Steve then noticed a small note next to the chute. He read it and it said:

To Steve
>    Meet me at 17 Gorthen Avenue – my house
From Markus

He sort of guessed he should be at 17 Gorthen Avenue, which was Markus' house, so he decided to go there. He took the note with him, and walked around the building, opened a gate, and closed it behind him.

It was a bit of a long walk, but it wasn't too bad.

When he got there, he saw that Markus was there watching the construction of his house.

"Hi, Markus!" said Steve just as he got there.

"Hi, Steve. I wanted you to come here because, well, to put it bluntly, I was told that Herobrine is going to summon his troops from the over world and the Nether, and he shall destroy Minecraftia. Cheery stuff, huh?" explained Markus as he made hand gestures to the borders of the city.

"Well, what should we do about it?" asked Steve.

"I don't know, but the mayor gave me a diamond sword, so I'm protected." Said Markus.

"I need to go buy some diamonds. Wait right here." Said Steve.

Steve ran to the general vendor and pushed open the door. The door wouldn't move. He tried pulling it and then it moved. He rushed inside and stood in front of the shopkeeper.

"I need to buy all your diamond, please." Said Steve.

"Well, okay. But only if you can open this mayonnaise jar. I haven't had lunch yet."

"Really? Okay then." Said Steve as he swiftly grabbed the jar and opened it with no trouble. "There. Now how much diamond do you have?"

"29 diamonds."

"Then I want to buy them all, please."

The person handed over the diamonds, and Steve rushed out the door.

"Thank you!" shouted Steve as he bolted away.

In a few minutes, he had made 2 sets of diamond armour, and a diamond sword. When he was done there, he sprinted back to Markus.

"Thanks for not leaving. I just needed to get some gear." Explained Steve as he gasped for breath.

With that, Steve handed Markus a mayonnaise lid.

"Huh? Why are you giving that to me?" asked Markus who looked completely dumbfounded.

"Whoops, sorry. Wrong pocket." Said Steve as he placed the mayonnaise lid in his pocket, and then took out a full set of diamond armour. "Here we go!"

"Thank you, I needed some of that." Said Markus, sounding very thankful. He put on the armour, and looked at himself in it.

"Now let's hurry. It can not be long until an army of enemies is here." Said Steve, as he started searching the sky.

"I agree." Replied Markus as he also searched the sky for tell tale signs of enemies. E.g., bombing, evil things flying around, etc. "Look! Up there! I see a... is it a creeper dropping from the sky?"

"Yes! I think it must be a creeper. It is green, and is hissing. This is not good. If they are falling from the sky… that means that the only flying enemy there is must be here! And they are the black fig…" said Steve, but he got cut off by Markus.

"They are called Endermen, personal bodyguards of King Ender himself. It means big trouble." Said Markus. He trailed off because he made another observation. "Wait a minute. The Endermen are leaving, now coming back. Oh! I know what is happening! They are just transporting the troops over to here! They are not really fighting!" Markus now had a little hint of relief and joy in his breath.

"Maybe not, but they are still transporting troops over here. Look, now they are taking skeletons!" said Steve, who wasn't really very relieved about the fact the Endermen were not fighting.

"I know! We could use one of the salvaged HPGCLBMBAEPs, maybe. The ender pearl that concentrates the beam would knock the ender pearl out of *them*. That is a good idea." Said Markus excitedly. He was obviously excited because he was jittery and jumping about.

"Okay then, which way to it?" asked Steve. He started walking in one direction already, but stopped and walked back to Markus.

"Follow me." Replied Markus who, now was no longer excited, perhaps a bit let down by Steve not following his excitement.

Markus walked down a road, turned left, passed the bakery, passed the general vendor, and then walked inside the butchers.

"Huh? Why are we going in here?" asked Steve. He scratched his head.

"I am a bit hungry." said Markus.

"How can you eat at a time like this? We are under attack!" shouted Steve. Steve could not believe that Markus wanted to eat something when the city is burning.

"No, not really Steve. Stand on that platform over there."

"This one?"

"No. The one next to it."

"Now, put your hand on the wall."

"Okay."

When Steve and Markus did this, the wall opened up and there was a very large room. It was dim, and the walls were painted a dirty sort of blue. The light looked like it was coming from space behind the paint, illuminating spots in it. In the middle of this very, very large room was a gun. It stood on a tripod, and had an ender pearl at the front of it. It filled up about ½ of the whole room.

"Is that the HPGCLBMBAEP? It looks big, and it has an ender pearl at the front." Asked Steve. He was looking at the room and gun in unspoken awe.

"Yes. That is the HPGCLBMBAEP. Salvaged from King Ender. Found it just laying around. It is the most deadly piece of weaponry against Endermen, creepers, zombies, skeletons and spiders. Although due to the spider's size, they often escape the blast. It takes two people to operate it. One to aim, one to fire, charge, and make sure the aiming doesn't eat up too much energy from the glowstone. When the glowstone dries out, it turns into gunpowder, and it will explode if you try to fire it."

By the time Markus was done explaining it, they were close enough to get in.

"Okay, Markus, you charge, fire, etcetera, and I will aim."

"Got it. I man the upper station, you man the lower station."

Markus climbed to the top of the weapon via really long ladder, and Steve stayed at the bottom.

"Wait! Before ignition, I have a few tweaks I want to make." Shouted Markus. He quickly opened the barrel and added some gunpowder mixed with creeper blood, some string soaked in spider blood, a bone, and an eye of ender. "Okay, this should make the laser target the enemies. Just in case you don't aim perfectly." Continued Markus.

"Thank you!" shouted Steve.

"Okay. Ignition in 3... 2... 1... ignition!" shouted Markus. The gun let out a loud roar, followed by a loud hum.

"Aiming now!" shouted Steve. He pulled the gun around to face an opening in the building that pointed towards the army of enemies. "NOW FIRE!!" shouted Steve.

With that, Markus flicked a switch, and then the gun started charging for 5 seconds, and then let out a deafening BANG sound that broke windows. The laser split up into 9 parts, or so Steve counted, and hit over 50 troops. In the mean time, Steve had been knocked against the wall, and Markus had fell about 10 meters onto the ground. He landed with as much of a thud that the machine made when it started up.

Markus was fine, though. His diamond armour had absorbed the shock. He got back up, and readied himself for another blast, while Steve jumped up to the bottom of the gun.

"Ready? I am aiming again!" shouted Steve. He started pushing it. "FIRE!" He fired a

second time, and the same thing happened. Steve and Markus fell off, and the beam split into 9 pieces. Except this time, the enemies were retreating. The creepers got forced up into the Endermen hands, and they all ran away.

The city was in ruins countless fires had appeared from the creepers' explosions.

"We did it! Yay! No more enemies!" said Steve.

"Yep, we did!" said Markus.

"Now, we better start cleaning up the city before the fire spreads.

# Chapter 13

King Ender was supervising the progress of his troops.

"Hurry up!" he ordered to his troops.

They were almost there. The Endermen were dropping off the creepers first. The creepers were falling down, and then they, most of the time, exploded on contact.

The only things that King Ender could see were flames, explosions, and two people dressed in shiny blue. He saw that those two people down there were Markus, his prisoner, and Steve, the could-have-been soldier if he was trained properly.

"Those people in the shiny blue: KILL THEM!" he commanded.

The two people there had flown into the butchers. Two Endermen flew down to kill them, but the mayor blocked the path.

"You will have to get through me first!" shouted the mayor, who sounded braver than he actually was.

In a second, the Endermen flew down to him and raised their hand as if to punch him, but in a flash, the mayor drew his sword and cut the head off one, and stabbed another to death.

"The mayor... I am embarrassed to be here with these rookies Endermen. Drop creepers over there!" shouted King Ender.

Suddenly 9 large laser beams fired from the dome next to the butchers, and hit most of the Endermen.

"More troops! We need to fall back! Retreat!!" shouted King Ender as he himself went ba
ck.

Another 9 laser beams fired and struck so many of the troops, it was only King Ender, (Who had himself a singed arm from the second blast) and 3 of his bodyguards. The rest were unconscious or dead.

When King Ender had returned to his castle, he sat down.

"Now, we need more ender forgers, and a mobile version of the HPGCLBMBAEP. Get to work!" said King Ender.

"THAT IS IT!" said someone, obviously daring.

"Who said that?" asked King Ender, using a softer tone than he felt, but it still sounded harsh.

"That would be me, your Enderman forger!" said the person, and they scuttled out of a room, and then appeared to be a spider.

"I am sick of your complete disregard for anyone's feelings! Especially mine! Is anyone with me?"

No one answered; they just hurried off their work.

"THEN I SILENCE YOUR NEVER ENDING SONG OF DISOBIEDIENCE!!!" screamed the Ender King. He lifted his hand, and then turned the spider inside out. Then he chained the spider to a wall via his guards. "You should have obeyed, and then you would not have been pinned to a wall with you internal organs hanging out! It is entirely your own fault."

# Chapter 14

Markus and Steve walked out of the last broken house they had just fixed. That was all the houses they needed to fix.

The Mayor came to thank them.

"Thank you, great warriors! And, you're not too bad at being a carpenter either! Ha! Thank you!" said the Mayor, very thankful because of all the 'thank you' and 'good job' involved.

"You are most welcome...uh... what was your name?" asked Markus.

"Oh, my name... that would be Old Peculier. I used to be a great warrior, but I have grown old before my time. Oh, well... I am going to stop being mayor soon. Giving up the chase to someone named Drexel Corbelhand. He seems nice, a bit bloodthirsty though." Old Peculier sat down on a wall next to him.

"Would you like to come with us? We are always welcoming new members to out 'team'. If you were once a knight, you could be of some help. I saw you fight off two Endermen with a sword. That is a heroic act." Replied Markus. He really wanted to have Old Peculier join them.

"Okay then! I would really like to join you! I know my way all around Minecraftia! 86 years of experience really gives good things." He said as he stood up. He already started walking to the gate.

"So then, Old Peculier, where should we go?"

"I have heard that the forces of King Ender have left a very large hole in the wall of the castle Jeet's hold, in Yerta, and creepers attack them every day and night. We should go over there to defend the breach while the carpenters can fix it. Every time the fix a bit, more gets blown up by use
of a creeper."

End of Part 1

Part 2
The Adventures

# Chapter 15

Markus, Steve and Old Peculier started walking. First of all, they went to the main gate.

"Hello, we would like to go to Yerta. Could you just sign us off the registries?" asked Old Peculier.

"Yes, I can. What are your names?"

"I am Old Peculier." Said Old Peculier.

"I am Markus." Said Markus.

"I am Steve." Said Steve.

"Okay, then. Give me 5 minutes to do the paperwork, and then you will be free to go. I will need all of your signatures, though."

"Ok then, do I just sign here?" asked Old Peculier.

"Yes, and your friends will sign just underneath."

"There we go!" said Old Peculier as he signed his name.

The other two signed their names on, and the guard welcomed them.

"Ok then, so, would you like directions to Yerta?" asked the guard as he shuffled through a folder.

"Yes, I would like that. I am new to Minecraftia so I don't know where to go." Said Steve before Old Peculier could butt in and say 'no, no directions' and then they would go off and get lost.

"Okay then…" said the guard as he pulled out a dusty map. "Here are the directions. There aren't many people going to Yerta anymore. I don't know why, probably just not trendy to go."

He gave them the map and wished them luck on their journey.

"Well, the guard was quite nice. He gave us a map!" said Markus, who was holding the map.

"I agree. Anyway, how far does it say it takes for us to get to Yerta?" asked Old Peculier. He tried to bend over to see the map, but could only see a squiggly red line.

"It says… 3 days. Well, a bit of a walk then. As long as nothing bad happens."

Replied Markus. He was a bit afraid that he just jinxed himself.

And, he did jinx himself. In a few seconds, a panther jumped out and jumped onto Steve. Steve started to push him off, but Old Peculier drew his stone sword and pierced the panther's tough skin around the torso, and it ran off, whimpering.

"Thank you, Old Peculier! I told you your talents would come in handy." Said Steve happily. Then his tone turned more serious. "And Markus, do not, I repeat DO NOT jinx us again."

"Sorry, I didn't know that jinxing works." Replied Markus.

"Yeah, well now you do." Snapped Steve.

They walked for a while, and just at sunset, they found a small booth.

"Hello? Who is in there?" asked Markus.

"It is me! I am here to make sure you can handle it out there. I will give you a series of tests, and if you pass, then I shall let you through. If you fail, I shall give you a piece of iron and I will have to send you back."

"Okay then, what is the first test?" asked Steve.

"You must, take this gravel and use it to build a pathway over the gorge."

The person handed them each 64 blocks of gravel, and showed them to a big pit.

Markus, Steve and Old Peculier stepped over there.

"Now you can start in 3… 2… 1… go!"

At that 'go' signal, they frantically built gravel paths that they could run across before it fell into the lava pit.

Old Peculier fell, but broke his fall on some falling gravel. He noticed a door on the side of the lava pit. He built over to it, and climbed up, and he got to the other side and finished the test.

"Well done! You were good, and Old Peculier, you found the secret passage, so you are now going to be able to skip all other tests. You can observe with me." Said the person.

"Thank you. What test do they have next?" asked Old Peculier.

"They have to kill a dragon."

"I think I will join in for this one, then!" said Old Peculier as he put on his helmet and drew his sword. Then he charged into the arena, and stood next to Steve and Markus.

"You have to kill a dragon in this test, guys." He said.

"Kill a dragon!? I am glad you are here to help!" replied Markus.

"Well, here it comes!" said Steve.

A large, black dragon emerged from a fairly large cage. It had purple eyes, and looked like an Enderman in dragon form.

"It is an Ender Dragon. The most feared being in all of Notch's kingdom." Said Old Peculier.

Suddenly the dragon charged at Old Peculier, but his stone sword dug deep into his ribs. The creature let out a pained roar, and bit Old Peculier on the arm.

Old Peculier fell back in pain, but managed to carry on. He quickly limped to behind the dragon, and the dragon was occupied by Markus and Steve who were hitting the dragon in the face, not really aiming or having any grace about the matter. Somehow though, they still managed to hurt it.

Old Peculier, in a new found burst of speed, jumped up onto the back of the dragon, and sprinted along its spine, and finally finished the fight with a stab in the head.

The dragon let out one last roar, and then majestically lifted it's wings and flew away.

Steve looked at Markus, Old Peculier, and then the dead dragon.

"We scared a dragon!" exclaimed Steve after a long silence.

"Yeah, we did, actually! Yeah!" said Markus as he poked the dragon to make sure.

They returned to the person who was standing outside, watching.

"Good job. You scared that dragon without too much wounding." Said the person. He made a little point to the open wound in Old Peculier's arm. "But this means you get the final challenge, and also the hardest. You must fight me in a 3 on 1 battle."

"Wow, you have a big ego!" exclaimed Steve. He didn't mean to say it, it just slipped out.

"Do you want to fight me?" asked the person as he drew his sword.

"Well, I see no reason not to." Replied Steve. He sounded brave, but his conscience was telling him not to fight him, as Steve was not an experienced fighter by a long shot. He barely just got to Minecraftia!

"Then we duel. 1 on 1, due to the arrogance of your friend." Said the person, who got a creepy grin on his face.

"Deal. I have been known for being an experienced warrior in my land!" bluffed Steve. He was on the verge of outright lying.

Suddenly, the person charged at Steve, bearing his sword high above his head, but Steve was too quick, and Steve ducked, made a painful blow to the knee caps, and sent the person toppling over.

"You have fought well so far, but the fight is not over yet!" said the person, who was trying to be very intimidating, and it worked.

Suddenly the person tried another charge, and this time Steve pushed the person with his free hand, sent him to the ground, and kicked his sword away. Now the person was at his decision to kill, or to let him go freely.

"You don't want to kill me." Said the person, who was carefully eying the sword at his throat.

"How could I benefit if I let you go, then?" asked Steve, waving his sword about his chest, nose and throat. "You would, what? Continue to stay here and challenge people who just want to travel? I don't think so. I will let you go if you promise never to challenge another soul who comes away from a town." Steve was now trying to sound as intimidating as the person who had intimidated Steve before the short lived fight.

"I promise…" said the person very cautiously.

"Promise what?"

"I promise that I will never challenge another soul who comes just to travel."

"If I ever find you here again, I shall kill you. Now run!" said Steve. He took the sword away from the person's throat. "RUN!"

At that, the person ran away.

"Good job, Steve! You showed him!" said Old Peculier. "Now let's continue our journey, we need to get there much more quickly."

"I agree, let us go with much haste." Said Markus.

Markus quickly walked to the front, in almost a jog. He was much further ahead than Steve and Old Peculier, because Steve just had an incredibly stressful 1 on 1 showdown, and Old Peculier, is, after all, a senior citizen, so he could no longer walk as fast as he would like.

# Chapter 16

After a very long walk, they found Yerta. Yerta was a fairly large place, with a castle wall around it. The castle wall must have been at least 100 meters high, if not more.

"There is Yerta!" exclaimed Old Peculier in fascination. "It has nice architecture, and nice castle. But is has not got so nice a history. This place was first built as a dead body storage facility. It was just a big mound of bodies. And then, the place got made out of stone to keep people from looting the dead bodies for grotesque experiments. And it worked, but then along came King Yert III, and changed it, so now it is a city, and there is a proper graveyard in there. Big graveyard, it is. And now, here it is! With a big hole in the rear wall, that gets invaded every 5 minutes. Not a great way to live."

They noticed a guard next to the opening just like the one in Minsoon.

"Hello guard. We came here to help with the breach, could you register us as in the city?" asked Markus.

"Yes, I can. Where did you first come from?" asked the guard. He was going to get a sheet of paper with a densely packed table.

"We came from Minsoon. I am Old Peculier, this is Steve, and this is Markus." Said Old Peculier as he gestured to both, Steve, and then Markus.

"Ah, the city of Minsoon! Good place, which is where most of my friends are. I have a few friends in Garson, but they are also having some difficulties. So then, are you, like wandering adventurers, doing good deeds for places and people in desperate need? Or did you just happen to hear that Yerta was in trouble with the breach?" asked the guard. He was talking in a fairly up beat tone.

"We apply to both, category one, and category two. We are adventurers who do good deeds and fight off evil and what not, but we also did just happen to hear about the breach in the wall of Yerta." Replied Markus.

"Alright, then! Here are the forms," said the guard as he handed them each a form. "Now fill these in, they are applications to be allowed to enter the city."

They each took the form and began filling it in. They scribbled down their initials, their signature, and days for their forms to be stored in the databases.

They all agreed to have their forms stored for 5 days, and then thrown away.

"Here are the forms, I hope they are all in order!" said Old Peculier as he handed the forms to the guard.

"Okay, then! I will let you in. Good luck on repairing the breach!" said the guard as Old Peculier, Steve and Markus entered the gates.

There was a very large, looming building over them that they had to walk through in order to get to the breach. The building was made of white-grey stone. The more they walked, the nicer it looked. There was and art gallery next to them, a gift shop with lots of small souvenirs and knick-knacks.

There was also a nice mural on the wall. It was space themed. It had happy astronauts floating through space, on mars, a happy, green, three eyed alien, and 5 point stars.

"That is a nice mural!" exclaimed Steve. He pointed to it.

"It is pretty nice." Replied Markus. He was obviously less amazed at it. "I like the simple colours and happiness everywhere, but they aren't wearing helmets! They wouldn't be breathing any thing!"

"I don't know, it's a mural, it doesn't always have to make sense!"

"Hmm, I guess you are right. Still doesn't seem quite right, teaching children you can breathe in space without a helmet on."

They continued their walk through the place. After a while, there was nothing to point out anymore, except reiterating that the floor was very smooth and nice against their tattered shoes.

"Very nice floor, this." Said Old Peculier, who was talking just for the sake of talking. "It does not erode my shoes at all! People who walk on this every day are probably wearing 15 year old shoes!"

"It isn't pure glassed marble, it is, in fact stone. It feels a bit rough in some places as well.

I am sure it does not wear out our shoes as quickly as cobblestone and gravel does, but it will wear it out. Don't drag your feet, because for all we know ours might be the only shoes in the whole city." Ranted Markus. He started scanning his own shoes, and then other people's shoes to see if they were in good shape or not. Surprisingly, they were in extremely good shape.

"They are shoes, I think that a city as well off as this will have good shoes for us. Really, they have an iron plated wall over there, and a gold mansion over there!" said Steve. He pointed to an iron wall, protecting some sort of nuclear plant, and then he pointed to a large, golden mansion. It glistened in the sun, and the reflections were casting bright yellow patches of light across the ground.

Coincidently, a shoe salesman passed them.

"Get your shoes here! Nice shoes! Only 2 gort! 3 gort for this lovely pair of shoes! They have a plastic outer casing, and they have a steel coating in between the fabric! Or how about this pair of stylish new shoes! High heels, with a pink glitter on the heels! With these shoes, you will be the envy of all your friends!" he shouted. He was holding two pairs of shoes over his head that he described. He walked over to Steve, Markus and Old Peculier swiftly. "You look like a nice man!" he said to Old Peculier. "Would you like to buy a hand made out of steel shoe? Or a sewn together patchy shoe, with a rubber bottom? Come on! I have a wife I need to feed!"

Old Peculier carefully observed the steel shoe.

"I would like to buy this shoe, here. It looks sturdy. How many gort is that?" asked Old Peculier as he reached into his pocket.

"For that one, the price is 5 gort, and it is a… how many of you are there? 3? A buy 2 get 1 free offer! So for 10 gort you can all get a steel footed shoe! Good deal, no?"

"Ok then, I think I have 10 gort." Said Old Peculier as he took out 1 token for 5 gort, and 2 tokens for 2 gort each, and 1 token for 1 gort. He handed the shoe salesman the money.

"Thank you, I need the money. Here are your shoes." Said the shoe salesman as he gave Old Peculier 3 pairs of shoes.

The shoe salesman hurried off to his house. His house was dirty, with many notices in the window about 'Unsanitary conditions – eviction notice'

"Well, now we really do have new shoes, so we are good to go on the adventure." Said M
arkus.

They walked out of the entry building soon. Suddenly, a person wearing a white, swirling hat appeared in front of them.

"Hello, my name is Skylord Lysander. I have come from the land of the Skylords to tell you something." Said the person, who is known as Skylord Lysander. "This place is a good place, but the people keep false promises. They are not at all trust worthy. The majority of people who live here are criminals, and they would love to get their hands on your wealth. Just be careful. I am a hologram, so I cannot aid you, but you will find me eventually."

Suddenly, a large person – no, Enderman grabbed Skylord Lysander and chucked him against a stone wall; causing a loud crack from his ribs. The hologram shut off, and then Steve, Markus and Old Peculier were left standing there, slightly bewildered.

"Um, do you guys know what just happened there?" asked Steve. He looked at Markus
    and Old Peculier.

"I could be wrong, but I think he meant whatever he just said. Do you think he meant what he said? I do." Replied Markus, with a very large amount of sarcasm.

Old Peculier nodded in agreement.

"Fine," sighed Steve. "But who is not trust worthy? Everyone? Someone? A handful of people? It just is very weird, because he didn't specify, and we were just going about our business, and he appeared out of no where."

"I suppose he did. He said we will find him, so don't worry! Just go about life as normal as if he never appeared. It doesn't *really* matter." Said Old Peculier. He very much took the attitude to just wave off the matter, and act, well, as he said, as if it never happened. "We must keep haste, because I have heard the breach is harder to defend…" Old Peculier trailed off. His eyes were locked on the sunset. "…at night" he said quietly.

"We must really start going with haste NOW!" said Markus as he started jogging to the breach.

He noticed that street lights were being turned on. Then he noticed the type of street light varied in different areas of poverty and richness; in the poverty-stricken areas, the street lights were just dim torches on a wooden pole. In wealthy places, the street lights are gold blocks, and on top a single block of glowstone, and in extremely wealthy places, the street lights are a string of diamond blocks, with a neat cluster of glowstone on top.

After running for a while, the street was only illuminated by the light of the street lights and the moon.

"There is the breach!" shouted Steve. "We need to call the carpenters to fix it while we defend it!"

It was mere seconds before they reached the breach, and when they did, Old Peculier noticed a creeper prowling around the area.

"Look! A creeper!" shouted Old Peculier as he pointed to a moving shadow. "It is trying to sneak around us! Steve, get it from behind, Markus, you go and start up the beacon!"

Steve crept behind the creeper and stabbed it, and it oozed out grey, slightly damp powder. Markus lit a large wooden tower on fire, and Old Peculier started getting supplies.

Suddenly, a wave of about 7 or 8 creepers came through the breach. Just the sound of all the hissing was hurting Steve's ears.

"Hurry up, guys! I can't hold on for much longer!" said Steve as he sliced a creeper in half.

"I am coming, Steve, just wait a minute, if this wooden pole will stay lit then I will join you!" shouted Markus.

"HURRY!" screamed Steve. He was losing ground to the creepers.

Then, as he backed away, he hit something. He turned around in shock, and was standing nose to nose with a creeper. He tried to run, but he was surrounded. Suddenly his life flashed before his eyes, and the creeper exploded. It sent Steve flying out of the castle, through the breach, and knocked his sword out of his hand. He opened his eyes for the last time, just to see his shattered diamond armour fall down his face and body. And then he fell dead.

"Steve?" said Markus when he found out that no one was keeping the creepers occupied. "Um… STEVE!!" he shouted, much more loudly. He banged the wooden pole.

He could feel the vibrations of creepers trying to climb, but not having any arms, so they couldn't. But instead they started shaking and bumping the wooden pole, to try to make M arkus fall. Before Markus could call for Steve a third time, his hand slipped and he swerved backwards. He continued to hold on with all of his might onto the wooden pole with his legs, but he slowly slid down. He drew his sword immediately, and waved it at the creepers.

He did manage to pierce the skin of the creepers, but the grey ooze inside them didn't fall out, so they kept on fighting. Markus plunged the sword deep into the skin of a jumping creeper that fell to the ground.

"Old Peculier!! I need help!" shouted Markus, but it was no use. Old Peculier was too far ahead, alerting the absent guards, to hear Markus.

Markus considered carefully. He would never get out of this place, probably, and he would just keep fighting for a lost cause. He has no real purpose here. And, if he sacrificed himself it would still save Steve and Old Peculier, because the creepers would blow themselves up. He thought about this, and then relaxed his legs, and he fell to the ground, where he instantly got blown up by the creepers. All the creepers blew up, just like a big firework show.

Old Peculier did notice that. He turned his head to see a huge amount of creepers go up into the air and explode, shooting more into the sky.

"Steve! Markus! Are you okay?" he shouted. There was no answer.

He walked a bit closer. Then a lot closer, then it turned into a panicked sprint.

"STEVE? MARKUS? HELLO?"

Then he saw shattered diamond armour, broken into a hundred crystals. He realised what just happened.

"Oh, no. Oh no oh no oh no oh no oh no. This is not good. I will need to fix the breach myself. The carpenters are coming, and the guards have been assassinated. Oh no." thought Old Peculier.

Then, about 4 carpenters came to the breach.

"You need to protect us. We can't fix the breach on our own, can we?" said a carpenter, who was clearly not aware that 2 people just died in protecting the city.

"Yes, okay. I shall." Said Old Peculier grimly, as he walked outside the breach.

He drew his sword, and started scanning the area around him. He saw some fading stars as the sun came up, and he saw the corpse of Steve, which he tried very hard not to look at.

There were no creepers during the whole time the carpenters were fixing the breach.

# Chapter 17

After the breach had been mended, Old Peculier realised that he had been built out. He couldn't get back in because of the big breach in the wall was mended. He also did not feel quite right digging underneath the stone wall, because if someone caught him at it, he would get quite embarrassed; and if a guard caught him at it, he could get into a lot of trouble.

He decided to walk around the city. He also decided to bring Steve and have a proper funeral.

It was a long walk, and there were several glass breaks in the monotonous tone of stone. He passed a desert; he passed grass land, a forest and a swamp.

However, he did finally get to the front gates. By the time he got there though, his feet were burning and aching as if his very bones were on fire.

"Hello," gasped Old Peculier. He bent over, and dropped Steve on the ground for a moment.

"Hello." Said the guard that Old Peculier was talking to. "How can I help you?"

"My name is Old Peculier, could I re enter the city, please?" he asked. At once, the guard sifted through a file. He pulled out a white piece of card.

"Okay, I think this is your form." Said the guard as he carefully inspected it. "Yeah, you can come through then."

"Thank you." Said Old Peculier. He walked through the gate, dragging Steve behind him.

Old Peculier got a lot of funny looks, probably because he was dragging a corpse through the city.

"What are you doing with that body?" asked one citizen. He kept a distance, being weary that Old Peculier could be a murderer.

"This is my friend, and he died. He got blown up by creepers, so I am going to give him a right and proper funeral."

"Oh, okay... but I will have my eye on you, what with the possibility of being a homicidal maniac."

After that brief exchange, everyone returned to their normal days work, but kept glancing over their shoulder in doubt every few seconds. Old Peculier walked down to a dark grey building, with a good bit of dust on small overhangs that only go out about an inch or two.

Old Peculier pushed open the door and dragged Steve inside. He then noticed that the building said 'Pete's Funerals', and underneath it said '*The best you can get, you know!*'.

"Hello? I have a funeral I would like to have planned." Said Old Peculier. He picked up Steve and painfully lumbered inside.

"Yeah? Who for?" asked the person behind the counter very bluntly.

"The name is Steve, and he died in a creeper battle."

"Okay, let me just get down the information." Said the person behind the counter. He filled in some letters on a sheet, and then tucked it into a thin slit on a machine. There was a very loud noise, as if the machine had turned the paper into stone and was then cutting it with a blunt saw.

In a moment, a slice of stone *had* come out, and it had the information about Steve on it. It said: 'Steve – A good man – lived in Yerta for only 2 days – Killed by creepers'

"Here is the tombstone – Bury him at crescent falls, at 11:00. Next!" shouted the person.

Old Peculier checked the time on his watch, and noticed it was 10:45. He made his way over to crescent falls.

Crescent falls was a large mountain, with a trickle of water that moved along a curve. It had many tombstones on it, and was packed full of bodies.

When Old Peculier got there, it was 11:00, so he dug a large hole. But then, he decided that there were many people in town who claimed they could raise the dead, so he abandoned the hole. He took Steve and left.

He walked for a while, until he came to a place called 'Niduki's Dead Rising'. He walked inside, and then saw a person behind the counter.

"Hello, I am Niduki. I can raise your dead." Said the woman. She had an arched back, and didn't look in the finest state of health.

"Yes, can you raise Steve from the dead?" asked Old Peculier as he put Steve back onto the floor.

"Hm, I shall try. Steve…" said Niduki

With that, Niduki opened a small crate, and pulled out a small potion. It was purple and was fogging up the potion with a purple smoke.

"This is a resurrection potion. It is said to have come from the soul of Notch when he came to Minecraftia and faced off with Herobrine, but he lost the battle, and instead of populating the Nether, Herobrine populated the Nether." Said Niduki. She carefully poured the cloudy liquid onto Steve's head, and in about five seconds, Steve drew a deep breath.

"Steve!" shouted Old Peculier as he ran over to him. "You have been resurrected!"

Steve made a mundane grunt, and then realized he had just been brought back from the dead.

"Yay! That is good! For an understatement, at least!" replied Steve after he snapped out of his trance.

"He lives! This is a joyous day, because sometimes it doesn't work..." said Niduki. "Now, pay up." She said that a bit more bluntly.

Old Peculier dug into his pocket and pulled out a few tokens.

"Here you go." Said Old Peculier as he gave the tokens to Niduki.

Old Peculier and the newly resurrected Steve left the place with a aura of joy around them. So much so, that a bystander burst out laughing after trying to contain their random joy.

"Now, I couldn't save Markus, because I couldn't even find his corpse. I don't know what even happened, but I assumed it was to do with the creepers." Said Old Peculier.

"Oh, yeah! We need to go and fix the breach in the wall!" exclaimed Steve.

"No, I took care of that. We don't need to."

"Oh. That's a really big relief, could you imagine if I died again??" joked Steve, who chuckled a bit at the thought.

"So, anything left to do here to your recollection?" asked Old Peculier as he stopped in his tracks at an intersection in the road; one way was leading out of the gates, and the other path was leading back into the city they were planning on leaving.

"Nope, I don't think so. Let's go." Said Steve.

Old Peculier and Steve, at this signal took the path to the right, which was the gate to exit. When they got there, the guard asked if they wanted to be signed off.

"Should I sign you off the register?" asked the guard. He knew them because they kept going to and fro the gates. "Well, should I?"

"Yes, please. I think that would be best. I don't want to have any license forgery or anything!" replied Steve, who was waking from the trance a bit more.

"Okay, then!" said the guard as he ripped up the form. He casually tossed it into a grey bin, and not all of the shreds went in. "Now, you better leave before the turrets detect as not on record, sorry to make you go so abruptly!" said the guard, who was carefully eyeing a ceiling mounted machine, about the size of his chest, and it was opening itself up to reveal a gun.

"Wait, I have an idea!" said the guard, and before the turret hooked its ammunition belt to the gun, the guard clipped a blue wire, exposing its sparking copper cord inside.

"There we go, now. I wanted to give you this piece of obsidian, to help keep away deadly spirits. There is one for each of you, so if a spirit from the Nether somehow escapes, it will be absorbed and then it will decompose inside this bit of obsidian. It is a bit heavy, so I can understand if you don't want to take it, but it *does* keep away Nether spirits, it works, I have tried it, so do you want it?" said the guard as he handed them each a black sort of purple material.

"Yes, I think it could come in handy." Said Old Peculier as he took it. He noticed it was colder than room temperature, as if it had been contained in a freezer. It also felt like a sort of rough glass.

"Yep, sure, I will be taking that!" said Steve as he took one as well.

With that, they thanked the guard and left the gates.

"Thank you, you may have just saved our lives!" said Old Peculier, who was thinking of the long term about if they really need one.

"Thanks guard!" called Steve.

"You are both welcome; I mined that myself! I do like a bit of mining here and there when I am not on shift." said the guard, who got back to his paper work.

Steve and Old Peculier had left the place, and were continuing along the current road until they came to some place.

# Chapter 18

Markus was once again in a very dark place.

"Ah, I see you have died again." said a voice that was presumably Notch.

"Yeah, sorry. I hate to bother you." replied Markus.

"Don't worry, I don't have much to do." Said Notch.

"So what is going to happen to me?" asked Markus who was getting a bit anxious about the consequences of dying twice.

"I am afraid I am not allowed to reincarnate you a second time, but I can let you live up here with me and the other people who have died." As Notch said that, a white door opened up from no where. "Or you can go and live with Herobrine, who destroys worlds and conquers everything..." As Notch said that statement, a red door with the sound of tortured souls opened up.

"I don't have to think twice about my decision, I would like to spend the rest of... however long I will stay with you." Replied Markus as he made his way to the white door.

"Good, I need more company. They keep saying things like 'Herobrine is cool, he does stuff!' but only a handful actually come to see me, and even fewer live when they go to Herobrine, because there is a big lava pit at the bottom of a large drop!" said Notch as he opened the white door further.

Markus walked through the white gate, and when he entered it, the white door closed behind him, leaving just being able for white to be seen.

Then Markus saw a blurry figure walk towards him, with a maple brown upper torso, and a dark blue lower torso. Then as the figure got clearer, the person had a maple brown *shirt* on, and dark blue trousers. His face had a surprisingly simple texture; it was just single black eyes, an open mouth and a beard.

"Hello, I am Notch. I am the one that millions of people all across Minecraftia worship, and I also founded Minecraftia. Hello, Markus! You look very neat and nice for a dead person, how did you die?" asked Notch, who had a friendly look on his face.

"I got blown up by about 20 or so creepers, but I was wearing diamond armor, so I died from internal bleeding." Replied Markus solemnly.

"Ah, that would explain perfectly undamaged clothes. Do you want some new ones? I have a pretty good wardrobe." Said Notch as he gestured to a wooden cupboard behind him.

"Hm, do you have a blue top and a light grey shirt?" asked Markus.

"I think so. Problem is I can't just whisk up anything I want anymore, because Herobrine has taken the power, have you ever heard of battle of the lower levels? I lost that one, and now Herobrine owns the lower levels. He calls it the Nether, but I would have called it the Skylands. He also now has more control over the over world than me, so there are monsters that come out at night. Not very nice if you ask Me." said Notch, who was really regretting losing the battle of the lower levels.

"Yeah, I have heard of that. But when the time is right, maybe you could summon all the people in Minecraftia to go to the Nether and take over? I mean, you could, right?" asked Markus.

"That is exactly my plan. But for now, I can't. Herobrine delivers my food every day. That is how much power he has over Me." said Notch, who was getting depressed by the conversation.

"Anyway, it is no use crying over what is already done, so, where are the other people?" asked Markus, who was aware that Notch was getting depressed.

"I told them to go for a minute, so that I could welcome you here!" said Notch. Notch had perked up a bit.

"Well, I would like to meet them, please." Asked Markus. He looked around in case anyone was already here. He didn't see anyone.

"Okay then. I shall summon them." Said Notch as he pressed a button.

When Notch pressed the button, Markus heard a buzzing sound in the distance, and saw a few other people come. Markus then realized that he had been inside an enclosed box when the walls of it opened, showing more and more people.

"Hi! Are you the new visitor?" asked one person.

"Yes, but I am not a visitor; I guess now I am a resident." Replied Markus, who was unsure if that was a good thing, or a bad thing, or a neutral thing.

"Ah, good! Welcome!" said another person.

"So who are you?" asked Markus to the one who had spoken first.

"My name is Griddian. I founded Minsoon, when I died it was just a tribal village, but now look at it! Rich as anything. So then, what is your name?" replied Griddian.

"My name is Markus. I was an adventurer, but the creepers put a nasty end to that."

"Yeah, a zombie got me. It had a midnight snack – on me. But the mighty Notch has healed my wounds, and now I am as good as new!" exclaimed Griddian. He was quite happy without his wounds and scars.

"Yep, it is quite good that Notch healed you, because if he didn't, you would have a bit bite taken out of you somewhere!" joked Markus. He chuckled a bit.

"Yeah, that would be absolutely rubbish! Wouldn't it? Could you imagine me like that?" joked Griddian. He bent in half laughing, and his face went bright red. He looked like a giggling beet.

"Om nom nom" he said, and he mimicked eating food, and then mimicked it falling out again. "Whoops! Om nom nom. Whoops!" This made him fall over laughing.

"Um… okay…" said Markus, who also started laughing a bit. He didn't find it quite as funny as Griddian did.

"Yeah, Griddian laughs at everything." Said Notch, who was trying to hold back a smile, but it was coming through anyway. "It also makes everyone else laugh around him. Good man, Griddian. Good man…" Notch trailed off.

Griddian finally stopped laughing. "So, want me to give you a tour?" asked Griddian kindly.

"Yeah, sure! I wouldn't mind." Said Markus happily.

Griddian started walking in one direction, and Markus followed.

"First, one of the major contributors to this place is someone call Mr. Rodgers, he wears a red, sometimes blue jacket and penny loafers, and very much enjoys having very, very, very lengthy conversations. He says he comes from the real world, but he died in Minecraftia, so he gets to be in our heaven. He has his own section of the place, and he calls it 'Mr. Rodgers Neighborhood.' It isn't a real neighborhood, but he likes it, and he lives there." Said Griddian. He pointed to a brown door.

"Could I visit him?" asked Markus, who really wanted to see behind the brown door.

"Yes, certainly. He likes visitors. Let's go." Replied Griddian.

Griddian walked up to the door, and pressed a button, and a beep sounded.

"Hello?" said a very smooth voice. "Who is it?"

"It is Griddian, and the visitor, Markus."

"Oh, good. Come in, then." Said the voice.

Markus made an obvious connection in his head. It was Mr. Rodgers speaking! Markus felt dumb as a doorknob.

The door swung open, and there was a fairly old man, but looked healthy.

"Hello, my name is Mr. Rodgers. Griddian, is this Markus?" asked Mr. Rodgers.

"Yes, yes it is. He wanted to visit you." Replied Griddian.

"Ah, yes. I always like visitors." Said Mr. Rodgers. He talked slowly and smoothly. "Won't you come in?"

"Okay then." Replied Markus as he stepped through the door, and into a plastic world, surrounded by plastic houses.

Markus followed Mr. Rodgers to a house, that he entered, so Markus followed.

"This is my neighborhood, let me tell you about it..." said Mr. Rodgers.

Markus listened intently.

# Chapter 19

When Old Peculier and Steve finally reached another city, they walked up to the guard.

"Hello. How may I help you?" asked the guard, who was sorting through files.

"What is the name of this city?" asked Old Peculier.

"The name of this city is Tropia, home of the Skylords. You are allowed to enter freely." Said the guard, in a very metallic way. It was as though he had said it a thousand times and it had lost its meaning and emotion.

"Hm, Tropia... never heard of it." said Steve. He was getting used to not knowing about places.

"Basically, this was established a short time ago, but it has taken resources from other parts of Minecraftia, and built itself up. There are quite a few redstone dust circuits, and the residents are fairly intelligent. Aw, who am I kidding? They are geniuses!" said Old Peculier, with his 'History Lesson' look on his face.

"I would like to visit them, then." said Steve, who was a bit excited to try and catch them out with a tricky physics question.

Old Peculier and Steve walked into the city, and saw many people who were all doing experiments, except one guy, who was kicking a sheet of paper into the ground with an angry look on his face.

They walked over to a building that says 'Quantum Physics Station'.

"This looks interesting…" said Old Peculier who was expecting not to be impressed by anything there. "Yeah… really, really interesting…"

"I am going to try to stump them." Said Steve with a very determined look on his face.

He walked into the building, and walked right up to the very first person he saw.

"How much do you know about quantum physics?" asked Steve.

"I know a lot. Do you want a lesson?" asked the scientist.

"No, no thanks. But can I try to catch you out?" asked Steve.

"You can try, but you can't." replied the scientist daringly.

"What is the equation for the electromagnetic force?" asked Steve.

"The equation would be $F(em) = k*Q*q/(r*r)$."

"Um… okay then…" said Steve, who had obviously felt very much beaten.

He left the building to go and meet Old Peculier who had been waiting outside.

"Yep, they are good with science, aren't they?" said Old Peculier. Old Peculier read the expression off of Steve's face.

"Yeah… what about the circuit place?" asked Steve, who wanted to see what they had come up with there.

"Just up ahead, see?" said Old Peculier, as he gestured to a building that was glowing red, but not with heat.

Old Peculier and Steve walked up to the building and entered it.

The building was a nice place. It had illuminated red walls, and was nice and warm. It was made of stone, except for the ground, which was covered with a velvet carpet. There was a little stall for robot sales. Some were made for cleaning, some for building, some for fighting, and some for defending. There was even one that was your personal servant.

"Let's buy a fighting robot, it could come in handy." Recommended Old Peculier. He walked over to the stall and looked at the various colors in which the fighting robots came. There were yellow, red, blue, green and grey or unpainted.

"Excuse me, could I buy a grey or unpainted robot?" asked Old Peculier.

"Um, yes. That will be 300 gort." Said the person behind the counter.

"Here you go." Said Old Peculier as he handed the person the money.

The person behind the counter wheeled a grey robot to the front of the counter, and then handed Old Peculier the instruction manual.

"Here is the manual. You will never know what to do without this. No, really. If you think you can just figure it out as you go along, you are definitely wrong."

Next, the person pushed the robot itself forward, flicked a few switches on it's back, and it turned on.

The robot had no head, more of a dome connected to the shoulders, with a glass lens that glowed red in the middle. When it got turned on, it instantly started talking.

"HULL IS AT 100%. SHIELD IS AT 100%. FUEL IS AT 50%. OPERATION SELECTED IS FOLLOW." blared the robot.

"Hm, good robot. Okay, thank you!" said Old Peculier to the shopkeeper

Old Peculier walked out of the building, and Steve followed.

"Wow, nice robot!" said Steve. "How much gun ammunition has it got?"

"Um… I don't know." said Old Peculier as he flicked through the manual. "Ah hah! Voice commands." Old Peculier cleared his throat. "Echo variable ammunition".

When Old Peculier said that, the robot looked at him.

"AMMUNITION IS FULLY CHARGED" said the robot as the light in the middle of the 'head' flickered.

"Charged?" said Steve in a very confused voice. "How can bullets charge?"

"I think it shoots lasers. Just a guess, I will ask it." Replied Old Peculier as he searched through his manual again. "Um, let's see... what about: echo system weapon."

"WEAPON INSTALLED: LASER RIFLE WITH 2.5064 GHz POWER."

"You were right; it is equipped with a laser rifle." said Steve as he inspected the hand of the robot, looking for any sight of a laser rifle. Steve could not find a glimpse of it.

"Yeah, I once owned a robot like this one, but it was a lot older. It moved incredibly slowly, and when it did move without jamming the cogs inside of it with the outer casing, it made a noise that sounded like a portable washing machine. With a megaphone. It was completely useless for defending a place, but it was good for farming and building. But that was a long time ago." Said Old Peculier. He was actually quite happy about getting rid of it, because he hated having to keep fixing it.

"So what happened to it?" asked Steve.

"Well, eventually I just couldn't stand the noise and fixing it, and all of the work to keep it from destroying the city, so I bought an iron bar, and smashed the robot to pieces. I used the pieces to make an iron house for me, and I used the iron bar to make my sword." Replied Old Peculier as he pulled his sword out of its holder to look at it.

"I see. Anyway, we had better get going. Don't want to be caught in the dark again, with all the monsters." Said Steve.

After Steve said this, Steve and Old Peculier started walking towards the gates. They passed all the buildings they had previously passed, and they got to the gates.

"Hello, we would like to exit this city, please." Said Old Peculier to the guard.

"Yes, sir. You may exit." Said the guard. He moved aside, and pulled a lever to open the gate. As he pulled the lever, Steve and Old Peculier, and probably the guard as well, heard a loud cracking sound. They realized that the sound had some from the gate, when the wooden poles that made up the gate were snapping against each other. The gate detached from the rest of the wall, and crashed down to the ground.

"Um… was that supposed to happen?" asked Steve, who already knew that the guard was going to say no.

"No." said the guard, very predictably.

"Do you really think that would happen on purpose?" asked Old Peculier in disbelief. "The gate just ripped itself off from the wall and crashed into the ground, oh, I know! The guard meant to do that!"

"I was just making sure…" said Steve.

"If you can make your way through the rubble without hurting or killing yourself, then you can go through." Said the guard as he picked up bits of broken wall and placed them back again.

"I think I might be able to do it. I mean, how hard can it be? I just need to hop through that bit there, jump over that, and either go around that, or just climb over it. And then I should be out!" said Steve, as he pointed at various areas of the rubble, and carefully planned out his escape.

"Yeah, I suppose that could work." Said Old Peculier, as he thought about it.

Steve walked over to the rubble and started acting out his plan to get out. He did as he said; he went through a bit of the rubble, he jumped over another bit, he climbed over the third and then he was out.

"Yay! I made it out of the rubble!" said Steve as he jumped up and down. "Come on, Old Peculier, you come next!"

"Fine, I will, but I won't like it." Said Old Peculier as he went over to the rubble and did the same as Steve did. "Hey, it works!" said Old Peculier as he jumped over the last bit of rubble.

When Old Peculier and Steve made it out of that last bit of random bad luck, then they continued to walk along the path that they were traveling.

"Let's keep walking. If we get to another city, then it could be very useful." Said Steve as he started walking very hastily.

"Yep, that would be good, considering there are about a million monsters out in the dark at night, we need a place to shelter." Said Old Peculier as he caught up with Steve.

After about an hour of walking, they came to a burnt down city. The city was blackened, and there were still small fires only just dying out.

"God, I wonder which city this was?" asked Steve. He slowly approached the city.

"I see a sign, maybe if we get closer I could dust some of the burnt parts off, and then I could read it?" said Old Peculier as he carefully walked towards it, being careful not to step on any burning embers.

Old Peculier started wiping the soot off the sign.

"Welcome..." read Old Peculier slowly. "To the city of... Minsoon?"

"Minsoon?" asked Steve in disbelief that so much could have happened after they left.

"Yes, Minsoon." Said Old Peculier.

"Who would have burnt down a city as nice as this one?" asked Steve.

"I don't think it was on purpose, I think it probably an accident at the forge. And with the new mayor, I don't think he got to the fire quick enough. Before we enter, I recommend that we set the robot to stay. OPERATION IDLE." Replied Old Peculier. Old Peculier stepped inside the gates, because all he had to do you get inside was to push them lightly.

Steve followed Old Peculier, and when he did, Steve noticed that there were still a few people who were still there.

"Old Peculier, there still some people there! They are in the holy church of Notch, I can see them through the window" said

Steve as he tapped Old Peculier's shoulder, and then pointed to the church.

Old Peculier searched the church windows.

"Yes, there they are. I see them, should we go inside? To help or ask them about how the fire started?" asked Old Peculier as he scoured the inside of the church more so.

"Well, yes, I think that would be the obvious thing to do." replied Steve, as he started walking towards the church. Old Peculier followed.

When they got to the door, Steve put his hand in front of Old Peculier's hand as he was about to just open the door.

"If you just open the door, then they could be armed. There are monsters that come out in the night, and if something randomly opened the door, then they would probably stab you or shoot you. I suggest we knock, and then call in." recommended Steve.

"Good idea." replied Old Peculier.

Steve knocked the door gently, and then called in.

"Hello, we are here to ask you questions about what caused the fire, and I am with your old mayor!" shouted Steve.

"Yep, I am here with him, can we come in? The fire has stopped mostly." Said Old Peculier.

"Come in, then." Shouted a voice from the inside.

Old Peculier and Steve, on this command, opened up the door, and saw most of the towns residents all packed up inside the church.

"Is this everyone in town?" asked Steve as he surveyed the crowd of people.

"No, some people in the town escaped before the fire spread a lot. But by the time that we noticed, the fire had spread over the exit, and so we couldn't get out. The church was the only place that was close, not blocked by fire and not made of wood, so we went here." Said the same voice, that was coming from a fairly short person, with a brown mustache, bald, and a was wearing a white vest that was now populated by little grey clouds of dirt and muck, and a pair of blue jeans.

"Who are you?" asked Steve as he studied the person, because Steve thought he looked slightly shifty.

"I am the blacksmith. I slave away at a hot pot of lava, while you go and ruin your armor carelessly." Replied the person, quite testily.

"Okay then, how did the fire start?" asked Old Peculier.

"It all started when the mayor just caught a crazy streak or something, and he had a large swig of vodka. Then, he had another. And another, and another. He was as pickled as a... um... pickle. And after that, just by a stroke of luck, all the lights went out at night. The mayor stopped the officials from fixing it properly, probably because he was so drunk. He wanted to make sure it was done properly. Anyway, he went and lit a match. He brought the match outside, and then started lighting the lamps back on, one by one. Next, a resident came up behind him asked him if he needed any help. For some reason, the mayor got really, really angry and threw the match onto the person, which ignited him. Just like any normal person would do, he started running around screaming like a headless chicken. He ran straight to the nearest river, but as he passed, he made a bit of straw catch the fire, and before you know it, the whole city was in ashes." Replied the blacksmith.

"I see." Said Old Peculier, who felt he got a bit more of an explanation than what he was expecting. "So, why did the mayor drink so much?"

"I don't know. Some people say it was because he was afraid of the enemies, and some people say it was because he could not handle the pressure. Some people even say that it was because he had a massive party, and he drunk a lot in the secret party. No body *really* knows. Just guesses." Replied the blacksmith.

"Well, the fire has stopped, so you can come out now. There are only a few little hot ash spots you have to be a bit careful of. Don't want you to burn your feet, now, do we?" said Steve as he opened the door even wider, so that the people inside could see the outside.

"And it has, as well!" exclaimed the blacksmith. "We can walk outside now! Come on, guys, the fire has stopped!"

"Yes, it has. No disrespect or anything, but why are you just quite so happy about it?" asked Old Peculier, who didn't feel quite so happy about the fire stopping. Obviously, he was very happy about it stopping, but everyone was acting like it raged on for weeks and weeks.

"You know what? I just don't know. But the city has stopped burning! And it makes me feel happy, so really I have no objection!" replied the blacksmith as he did a little dance.

"Well, I suppose it is a fire, and fires can be pretty scary. So, I am guessing that it is that." Said Steve to Old Peculier. "I was once in a fire, but to be honest, it wasn't too bad. It was a fairly small fire, and I had a good bit of water to put it out. No body I could see was injured, but the kettle and the refrigerator were burnt to a crisp. But, then in the morning, I went out and bought a new kettle, and a beer bottle refrigerator. We didn't use the fridge much, so we could get by on that."

"Okay, so what should we do now? Should we help to rebuild the city of Minsoon? Or just leave and find somewhere else to go?" asked Old Peculier as he looked at the burnt city, and then the gates.

"Well, it is their city, and they built it in the first place, so it shouldn't be too bad. I mean, all they need to do really is just go out, find a tree, punch it down and build a house out of it. And maybe they could make them out of stone, to prevent this sort of incident from happening again." Replied Steve as he made his way through the city towards the gates.

"I suppose you are right on that. It is their city, after all." Said Old Peculier very unsurely. He wanted to stay, but he also wanted to go. He made up his mind a bit more. "Yeah, okay. Let's go!"

Old Peculier and Steve exited the city. When they were leaving the gates, they saw their robot. It had been in defense mode. It had it's laser gun equipped and deployed, and there was a couple of zombies and a skeleton on the ground with a significant burn mark either in the head, or in the body. Either way, it was fatal.

"OPERATION FOLLOW." Shouted Old Peculier at the robot. Instantly, the robot's gun folded up, leaving only a stump of a wrist on one hand, and he started moving.

"So, are we still moving along this path?" asked Steve.

"Yes. We need to find somewhere else. Remember Skylord Lysander? We need to find the land of the Skylords."

"OPERATION REMOTE SELECTION IS TRANSPORT TO LAND OF SKYLORDS." Blared the robot, as it's chest expanded and opened two seats.

"Well, we could walk, or we could sit on these seats sticking out of a robot's chest. Well, I am choosing the robot." Decided Steve as he sat on the left hand seat.

"I guess I will go with you, then." Said Old Peculier as he sat on the other seat, next to Steve.

When Steve and Old Peculier were both in, the robot's lower torso somehow propelled itself into the air, dragging the upper torso with it.

"Oh, god, this is not what I expected at all!" exclaimed Steve as he noticed the ground becoming further and further away.

"MAXIMUM HEIGHT." Blared the robot.

The robot suddenly fell to the ground. When it landed, a small thruster on it's foot fired up, and let it calmly fall to the ground.

"DESTINATION REACHED." Said the robot.

Steve and Old Peculier jumped off the robot very quickly.

"Wow, a bit more turbulent then I thought." Said Old Peculier, his eyes were as wide as watermelons.

"Yeah, just a little. If by a little, you mean a lot. And if by a lot, you mean OH-MY-GOD-MY-BRAIN-OOZED-OUT-MY-EARS." Replied Steve, as he mimicked having his brain melt. He clutched his head, and fell to the ground. When he got back up, the robot once again spoke.

"DESTINATION IS LAND OF THE SKYLORDS."

"Yes, I think we know that. OPERATION FOLLOW." Said Old Peculier to the robot.

The robot started following.

Steve and Old Peculier wearily walked into the city, making sure there were no traps or anything. There were no plainly visible traps, but there was a guard.

"Hello, how may I help you?" asked the guard.

"I would like to enter the city, please." Replied Steve.

"Me too!" said Old Peculier, who didn't want to have to go through a process twice.

"Okay, do you want to fight?" asked the guard.

"What? No, why?" asked Steve, as though the concept of fighting was as absurd as if he was applying it to Gandhi.

"Has no one told you?" asked the guard in genuine surprise.

"Told me what?"

"About Herobrines army being sanctioned here!"

"Definitely not! We were told the Skylord Lysander was here. We want to free him. OPERATION IDLE." Said Old Peculier.

"Skylord Lysander! Well, good luck freeing him! You'll have to bring down the whole enemy base if you want to free him!" said the guard. "Here, I will give you a map on his positioning. Many people have attempted to free him, but none have succeeded."

Steve took the map, and looked the guard in the eye.

"I have killed many a monster, and if this is just another lot of enemies, then I will kill many of them as well, until they flee. Hear me? I shall return with Skylord Lysander by my side." Said Steve. "And this is my friend, the mayor of Minsoon. He has killed an Enderman with a mere blow from his sword."

"Well, good luck. You will need it." Replied the guard as he opened the gate.

When the gate opened, Steve and Old Peculier saw a very large castle wall, made out of a dark, purple-red brick.

"Bloodstone. Or the elemental name, Netherack. It comes from the Nether, from Herobrines land. This is one of his settlements, obviously."

"Well, is that where we have to go?" asked Steve in dismay.

"Yes, I am afraid so." Replied Old Peculier.

Steve and Old Peculier just stood near the entrance of the city for a while, and then they started to grudgingly make their way towards the giant wall.

When Steve and Old Peculier got to the wall, they found that the wall was very rough when they touched it.

"Netherack, but even though it has been refined into brick, still rough and gritty." Said Old Peculier as he moved his finger around on the wall.

"Yep, thought so." Replied Steve as he tried touching it, also.

Steve took a breath, and opened the door. Immediately, when he opened the door, a wave of cold air engulfed him. He slowly stepped inside, and saw many creepers, skeletons, Endermen, spiders, zombies, everything evil. They were swarming the place, that was a large open space, and the castle was just over through a little walk..

"Wow. That is a lot of enemies." Said Steve as he looked at all of them.

Immediately, 3 creepers, 5 zombies and an Enderman all targeted him. The Enderman made it to him first. With a swift blow of the sword, the Enderman's arm got cut off. With a couple of more blows, the Enderman was in multiple pieces, and dead.

Old Peculier then entered the castle, and swiftly drew his sword. He drew his sword in good timing, as well. Because as he drew it, his sword sliced through the feeble, rotting flesh of two zombies. He quickly pieced his sword through the body of a creeper, and pulled it out again, through the side of the creepers body; leaving a very large slit in it's side, where all the ooze from the inside drips out.

Steve could not easily catch up to Old Peculier's death toll. Within a few surprisingly graceful blows, a lot of the enemies were dead.

"Wow, that was good." Said Steve as he killed another enemy. It was a skeleton, and it was killed *just* as it loaded it's bow with an arrow.

"Yeah, I used to practice!" replied Old Peculier, as he, himself fought a great number of them.

A number of enemies around the area were dead, but there were more coming.

"Hurry! We need to get to the castle!" said Steve. The gate was only opening for reinforcements, and it was closing quickly. They would need to kill every enemy that is coming for them, if they wanted it to open a second time.

With a flurry of swords, missed explosions from creepers, and arrows from skeletons, they managed to get through the gate while many more of them poured out like ants.

"We are in! Yes!" exclaimed Old Peculier, whose moment of joy was very short lived.

Before Steve could join in the celebration, he saw that there must have been thousands and thousands of prisons, all containing angry people.

"You can't do this to me!" screamed one person.

"I... can... do... whatever I... like!" said an Enderman. The Enderman grabbed the person by the throat and threw him against the wall. "Let... this... be... a ... warning to... you... all!" As the Enderman spoke this, he turned around and looked at all the other prison cells. His eye caught hold of Steve and Old Peculier. Steve and Old Peculier cringed when the Enderman's icy stare was cast upon them. "What... are you... doing... here?"

"Well, um, I don't... um," stuttered Steve.

"I don't... care!" shouted the Enderman as he teleported over to them, grabbed them, and took them to a small grey room. "Man flesh! All... the... same."

There were a lot of other people also in that room, and they all looked quite torn up.

"Better get in the line, you don't want to miss your tag, do you?" asked one person tiredly.

"Tag?" asked Old Peculier as he walked to the back of the line.

"The tag tells you which jail cell you will be in." replied the person.

"Oh, okay. I see." Replied Old Peculier. "So, we are going to stay in this jail. How lovely, you really can tell that Herobrine cares about your comfort, can't you?"

"Yeah, well, you'll just have to live with it. I am not saying you have to like it. Besides, if you keep making comments like that, they'll beat you to death!" exclaimed one person quietly.

Old Peculier fell dead silent. After a fair while of waiting, the line had diminished to Old Peculier's turn.

"Name." rasped an Enderman

"Old Peculier." Said Old Peculier glumly.

"Your... your... *cough* number... i-is... *cough* 52... 32. *cough*."

"Thank you." Said Old Peculier. He took the ticket bitterly, and very slowly walked to his cell. He could hear Steve behind him taking his ticket.

"Old Peculier!" called Steve.

"Yes?" replied Old Peculier as he turned , only to find that Steve was walking swiftly towards him.

"Wait! What is your cell number?" asked Steve, as if there was a very important reason.

"Um," replied Old Peculier as he checked his card. "5232. Why?"

"Because they will kill everyone whose number is below 4999!"

"How do you know?" asked Old Peculier. He was very glad that his was 5232, not 4232 or 3232.

"I heard some Endermen talking behind the prison registry office!"

In an instant, a loud crashing sound made Old Peculier and Steve look to their right. They saw a giant mechanical arm, made out of a purple material, that looked to be melting. It went high up into the air and came down very suddenly on top of a lot of prison cells. The prison cells were crushed, leaving only a lot of wiry rubble, and a very flat piece of metal. The arm continued to destroy that row of prison cells.

"Wow, I see how they are going to execute the people!" exclaimed Old Peculier, who realized he had stopped walking. He started walking quite quickly now, to make sure he didn't get beaten. After they walked for a while, they got to their jail cells.

"Well, this is my jail cell." Said Steve as he stopped at jail cell 5233.

"And mine is right next to yours!" exclaimed Old Peculier quite happily. "Well, I am as grateful as I can be about being in an Enderman jail, about to die any minute. When you think about it, it really, really sucks."

"I agree. We had better get in before the Endermen kill us." Recommended Steve.

"You're right." With this, Old Peculier and Steve stepped into their jail cells.

When they shut the doors, there was a loud clanking noise, and they noticed they had locked.

"Steve, can you hear me?" whispered Old Peculier against the stone wall.

"Yep, I can hear you." Whispered Steve, like Old Peculier just did.

"Good." Said Old Peculier, and then Old Peculier slouched back against the wall of his prison cell.

# Chapter 20

"Feeding... time!" rasped and Enderman, as it banged a large bead against the bars.

Old Peculier woke up drowsily. He didn't mean to fall asleep.

The Enderman threw a slimy, white, jelly at Old Peculier.

"Euch..." exclaimed Old Peculier a bit louder than he intended.

"What... did.... you... say?" asked the Enderman as it turned around angrily. It started emitting purple smoke.

"Nothing, just... nothing." Replied Old Peculier more quietly.

The Enderman's arm reach through the gate, and grabbed Old Peculier by the cheeks.

"If I... had... it my... way... you would... would be... dead... by now!" said the Enderman. It's grip on Old Peculier's cheeks tightened, until the Enderman got tired and threw him to one side. Old Peculier got a nasty scratch on his arm.

The Enderman continued to deliver disgusting slop to the other people in the jail cell.

"Old Peculier!" called Steve from the other jail cell.

"Yes?" he replied

"What is this stuff?"

"I don't know, but it feels like some sort of cow cartilage. Pretty gross!"

"I think I will save it until such time as I am starving to death."

"Yeah, sounds like a plan."

Old Peculier hid his white jelly in a small hole in the wall, that was an opening for him to store small things in.

"Hey, Old Peculier?" asked Steve, as he knocked on the wall.

"What?" replied Old Peculier.

"Do you suppose that this would be the place that Skylord Lysander is kept? You know, in the city of Skylords?"

"Yes, I guessed that. I also forgot about him. We need to figure a way to get to the button over there, by the rear exit." As

Old Peculier said this, he gestured to a red button, and on top of it, it said 'Emergency Cell Release Button'.

"Good idea, but how do we get out?" asked Steve, as he fingered the lock.

"Well, not to brag, but I spent 2 years in a lock picking with fingers class, and I was the top of my class."

"Good, so get out, pick my lock, and then press the button over there."

"Can do, but I won't pick your lock, because it will slow me down, and I will only free you again in a minute."

Old Peculier immediately started frantically working at the lock to his jail cell with his fingers and bits of chipped off stone. Within seconds, the lock was picked and it fell to the ground with a fairly loud clank. He cringed, to make sure it didn't alert anyone, and it did not. He carefully opened his gate, and made a sprint to the red button. This did catch one Enderman's attention. The Enderman started running towards him, and then teleporting. Old Peculier's fingers just brushed the button, and he flung his whole body weight onto the button. It pressed down, and all the cells flew open.

But, the Enderman had caught up with him. It grabbed Old Peculier, and started biting him. But Old Peculier was swift, and he managed to duck out of the way of the rotten teeth of the Enderman. Old Peculier grabbed the Enderman and drew his sword, he then pushed his sword into the Enderman's chest, leaving the Enderman limp.

Old Peculier noticed, to his dismay that all the troops in the castle must have come to fight, and fight they did. Fortunately, there were many Skylords, who appeared to be heavily experienced fighters. They killed many Endermen, many creepers, many zombies, skeletons and spiders, too. The rest of the people were either cowering, or staying in their cells in hope of not getting hurt.

"Old Peculier! Steve!" called a voice. "Over here! By the exit!"

Old Peculier started running to the exit.

"Hello? What is it? Yes?" replied Old Peculier.

"Hello?" called Steve, who appeared from the crowd of people.

"It is I, Skylord Lysander!" called the person, who was obviously Skylord Lysander.

They saw someone by the exit, their hand above their head, calling them.

"Come over here!" he called.

When they eventually got over to Skylord Lysander, they stopped for breath.

"My name is Skylord Lysander Griple, son of Trúr Griple. What is your full name?"

"I am Steve Persson, son of John Persson."

"I am Peculier Georgius, son of Mabel Georgius."

"Nice to meet you, Mr. Persson, and Mr. Georgius. I am a Skylord, a highly trained professional swordsman, and I hope I can be of some help in your quest."

"I am almost certain that you can be of much help to us." Replied Steve.

"I agree, we need more people to help kill Herobrine."

"Kill Herobrine, you say?" said Skylord Lysander, who was obviously extremely surprised at the weight of the mission they were carrying out. "You will need more than three people to help you with that!"

"I know, we have spread the word to the military officers in Yerta, and Minsoon. Could you help us to spread the word to the military officers in this place as well?" asked Steve.

"Yes, maybe. Jasper! I need you to deliver a message." Called Skylord Lysander. When he called, a man jogged over to him, avoiding a nearby creeper's line of sight.

"Yes sir?" asked Jasper.

"I need you to notify the military officers about this message." Said Skylord Lysander as he tucked a note in a bottle into the shirt of Jasper. "Good luck."

With that, the man jogged off, through the exit, and was on his way.

"Done. Jasper has never failed me yet to deliver a message."

"Good, Skylord Lysander, have you brought a sword?" asked Old Peculier, eying the holster, suspecting a positive reply.

"Yes, as a matter of fact I have. The best sword there is, a Skylord sword, forged in the mighty lands of Notch's Kingdom. It's glow alone will ward off enemies, to some extent." He replied eagerly.

"Very nice sword. Let's go along the path, to get to more cities." Said Steve as he made his way to the exit.

"Mr. Persson!" shouted Skylord Lysander. "Wait! Before you go, you should know that there aren't any cities left. They have either been pillaged, or never existed."

"Oh, so where is the rest of the country?" asked Steve as he walked back to Skylord Lysander.

"They have moved to the Nether, Herobrines country, where there is lava and fire everywhere, and never going out. Either by force, or because the over world is getting too dangerous for them. We need to find a hellgate to get to them. I know where one is, we just need to get out of here." Warned Skylord Lysander.

"Okay, let us go for real this time." Said Steve as he exited the place.

Old Peculier and Skylord Lysander were close behind.

"We need to go to Yerta, where the hellgate is. It is our only way to safely get into the Nether." Said Skylord Lysander, as he continued to walk along the path

End of Part 2

Part 3
The Nether

# Chapter 21

When Steve, Old Peculier, and Skylord Lysander got to the hellgate, they stood in front of it in silent awe for a minute or two.

"Are we going to have to go through that thing?" asked Steve nervously.

"I am afraid so, Mr. Persson." Replied Skylord Lysander.

"Aw, not good." Said Steve.

"I know…" said Old Peculier, as he trailed off.

They stood there for about ten seconds more, and then Skylord Lysander piped up.

"Mr. Persson, Mr. Georgius, we must proceed. I shall go first."

"By all means!" said Steve, as he stepped back.

"Yes, go on… definitely." Said Old Peculier as he realized that he was going to be second.

Skylord Lysander stood on top of the obsidian frame, and felt a wave go through him. The portal fell like a moving, cold jelly. It distorted his vision, things blackened out, they wobbled, all he could see was purple jelly twisting and swirling before his very eyes. He faded out of sight, and the portal let out a 'whoosh' sound.

"Okay, now me." Said Old Peculier as he stepped up to the portal, and stood on the frame, so that the portal was all around him, touching his body.

The world turned into purple swirling jelly, from Old Peculier's point of view, and he, too was off.

"Well, just me to go!" said Steve to himself as he walked into the thick consistency of the purple portal.

Steve, Old Peculier and Skylord Lysander had reappeared in the portal frame together.

"We made it through, that is a good thing. Now we know we haven't died from the travel to the Nether." said Old Peculier, unsurely.

"Don't jinx us, now we could die from long time effects of the portal, or the poison hasn't set in yet, or anything! Just don't jinx us." Replied Steve.

"I do not believe in jinxing, so therefore it shall not happen to me. Let us go to see who is in charge of this base, shall we?" said Skylord Lysander to both, Steve and Old Peculier.

The place they had teleported into, was a white building, made out of iron, that looked vaguely like a space station. It had a few doors, and a few just plain corridors. There were plenty of signs around, saying positions, places, where the corridors lead to, and all that sort of stuff.

"It is like a space station!" exclaimed Old Peculier, who noticed the way it had been put together.

"I agree. They erected it, expecting that this was a portal to the moon, because people had established a connection to the moon, and were hoping to go there. They built the portal, and went through it, but when they came out the other end, they just found a lot of lava, and burning things. At first they though that it was the moon, and the fire and lava caused the brightness of it, and the over world's atmosphere messed up the red color. And so, they erected the moon base. But when they realized that they were not on the moon, they built more appropriate bases for the Nether, but they didn't tear down the moon ones." explained Skylord Lysander.

"I see, that does make sense." Replied Steve.

They walked through the station for a while, and then they came to a room, with a lot of chairs. On the wall, it said 'Lobby – Waiting Room'. They took this as saying it was the lobby, or the waiting room.

"Well, I assume that we sit here, and press this button, and wait until someone comes to us." Said Old Peculier.

Steve pressed the button, and then he sat in a seat. It was fairly comfortable, it had a felt coating, but it had fairly stiff filling. Old Peculier and Skylord Lysander sat down next to Steve.

"Hello, how may I help you?" asked a women standing next to them.

"We would like to go to a city, we don't know which one. We are raising an army to overthrow Herobrine." Replied Skylord Lysander.

"Hm, army, ay? Because I see about a thousand people a day, so I could pass on a flyer about it, or something." Replied the woman.

"Yes, good idea..." said Skylord Lysander as he took a crumpled up piece of paper from his pocket and began frantically scribbling down: 'Army – now recruiting – going to kill Herobrine – to join, spread the word about it, and meet me in The End when I send the signal.'

"What is The End?" asked Old Peculier curiously.

"The End, is where the Endermen first started. It is Herobrines own land. The most dangerous place in the whole of Minecraftia. If we want to kill Herobrine, that is where we should go." Replied Skylord Lysander.

"Oh, I see." Replied Steve.

"Oh, sorry. Here is your note. Here you go. Please photocopy this and send it to other people." Said Skylord Lysander.

"Thank you. I will. To get to your nearest city, that would be, ooh. I think it would be Morgúul. It is an okay city. Not great, got a bit of damaged building." Replied the woman.

"Okay then." Said Steve as he got up, and walked over to a horizontal glass tube.

Old Peculier and Skylord Lysander followed him.

"So, how do we open it?" asked Old Peculier.

"Well, Mr. Georgius. I think that, judging by the sign, I say that we use the screen to choose our destination, and follow the instructions that we are given." Replied Skylord Lysander.

"I see. I shall do it." Said Steve as he went over there and started using his finger to select options. Soon, the glass door slid open, and there was a little glass capsule inside. Steve stepped inside, and Old Peculier followed. Skylord Lysander then carefully entered. Skylord Lysander pressed a button, and the door closed. Within a few seconds, they were moving extremely fast. And then, within a few seconds, they stopped, completely instantly.

"Hm, how strange. The momentum should have thrown us against the glass with such force it should have broken." Said Skylord Lysander, checking the glass for signs of stress and fracture. He didn't find any, so he entered the room it took him. He found it was not a room, as much as it was a very large castle. Made out of netherack bricks. That was a sure sign that it was one of Herobrines settlements.

"The-the..." stuttered Steve, not expecting it.

"Yes, I know. It must be one of Herobrines settlements." Said Old Peculier.

"Oh, no. And it is in the Nether, so it is even stronger." Said Skylord Lysander as he noticed a zombie pig man.

"What is that?" asked Steve as he pointed to the zombie pig man.

"That, my friend is a pig man, but he has caught a zombie virus, and is now a zombie pig man. As long as you do not attack him, he will not attack you, and it will be fine. But if you attack him, then he will call his friends and attack you with an army of zombie pig men. They aren't a nice force to tangle with. Just be careful." replied Old Peculier, recalling the last time he had seen one of these. It had been lost, and exited the realm through a hellgate.

"Okay, but why did it just dump us here?" asked Steve, who also noticed that the screen had turned off.

"Let me have a look, Mr. Persson." Said Skylord Lysander as he checked the wiring for signs of physical hacking. "I see... something has massacred these wires. They are in a mess. All touching each other, all cut in half. This is not the work of a random kick, or bump. This was deliberate, by someone who wants us to fail. Probably the work of a technical droid, that has been turned against us. It cut and fixed all the wires together."

"So, someone knows of our travels, and is trying to stop it?" asked Old Peculier.

"Yes, someone does. From now on, we must mask our identities. No more telling people our real names, and no more drawing attention to ourselves." replied the Skylord, as he stood up from checking the wires.

"I see." Replied Steve, as he thought about what he would mask his name as. "Would I be better as Jonathan, or Clive?"

"That is not a matter for us now. We shall use a different name for each person we meet." Replied Skylord Lysander.

After Skylord Lysander stepped outside the glass capsule again, an explosion made Old Peculier and Steve fall to one side.

"Ghast!" shouted Skylord Lysander. He saw a large white jellyfish hover above him, menacingly. "Come and get me, you foul spawn of Herobrine!" As the mighty Skylord said this, he drew his sword. It glowed bright white, and it cast a shadow, visible on the far wall of the Ghast.

The Ghast screamed and shot another explosive fireball. But when it came to Skylord Lysander, Skylord Lysander knocked it away to hit the Ghast. It screamed again, but the rebound fireball missed, and hit a large amount of netherack.

"Skylord Lysander!" shouted Steve as he got up from his hunched position, and ran over to him.

"Get back, you have no chance to fight a beast like this one! It would kill you in an instant!" shouted Skylord Lysander as he waved his free arm, to indicate him to go away.

"That is a risk I am willing to take, I am afraid!" shouted Steve back at Skylord Lysander. Steve drew his sword, and entered the fight.

The Ghast looked at them, very unsure about the output of the fight, for it's end.

Steve swung his sword at it. But it threw a fireball at his swords, that knocked the sword out of his hands.

"I told you that you were no match for a true warrior like me!" boasted Skylord Lysander.

Skylord Lysander jumped into the air, and then jumped off against a nearby wall of glowstone, plummeted through the air, and finally stuck his sword right through the Ghast. The Ghast screamed once more, and fell to the ground.

"See, what did I tell you?" asked Skylord Lysander as he got off from on top of the Ghast.

"Actually, you didn't tell us anything." Said Old Peculier, who just sat and watched the whole thing.

"Well, it isn't a problem. Now I am telling you." replied Skylord Lysander triumphantly, as he looked at the corpse of the Ghast. Within about ten seconds, the Ghast's body melted, leaving only some gunpowder behind.

Old Peculier stood up from his little mound of netherack, and walked over to where Steve and Skylord Lysander were standing.

"So, where to now? Asked Old Peculier.

"Well, hopefully we can go back, using the glass capsule." Replied Steve.

"Even if you could fix it, you still won't have any chance. Look at where it… was." Said Skylord Lysander, as he gestured to a large hole in the wall. It was smoking, and had many large splinters of glass in it.

"Oh. What about if we just jump into another part of it?" asked Steve as he stood on his tip toes to try to see over a large wall of netherack.

"We would need to catch another hacked capsule, and have it still be fixed, and jump into it. Besides, the next station could not be for miles! Tens and tens of miles! We just have to walk and hope we get lucky." Replied Skylord Lysander.

"I agree. Let's go." Said Steve as he started walking along the place where the tube leads.

They started walking in a direction. They walked for ages, and then they got to an enormous break in the path. There was a dead vertical drop, down to lava.

"Yeah, my luck. How do we get passed that?" asked Steve, as he looked down, to the bottom of the pit. The lava was bubbling, and even though it was so far down, he could feel it's heat burn his face, and dampen his brow.

"Wait, I have an idea. I can use some slime balls I received as a gift from my relatives. If I stick it to some netherack, and stick more netherack to that, we might just be able to get across!" exclaimed Skylord Lysander.

"Good! Start sticking and placing, sticking and placing!" said Steve, as he backed away from the edge quickly.

Skylord Lysander quickly and easily placed all the bits down, and made a thin bridge.

"Okay, everyone! Start walking, but only one at a time. I don't know how many people it can hold, or what the weight limit is. This slime is pretty strong, but I don't know how strong. Be careful! I'll go first!" said Skylord Lysander as he carefully made his way to the other end.

He was about half way there, when he heard a threatening crack.

"Oh no…" he muttered.

The crack was coming from right in front of him. He was torn between making a run to the other side, or making a run back to the other end, or staying where he was, so he danced around on the spot. However, this made the crack widen, and eventually split the bridge in two pieces. Both ends of the bridge were dangling down, towards the lava.

"Skylord Lysander!" shouted Old Peculier, as he ran over to the place where Skylord Lysander was hanging.

"Leave me! You can carry on the quest! Just stand on the dangling end, and jump!" shouted Skylord Lysander.

"No! As long as you are alive, I will save you!" said Steve, who only just realized the situation, as he was looking for more netherack to stick to it to make it thicker and stronger. He ran over to join Old Peculier's side.

"Then I am afraid I will have to rectify that." Said Skylord Lysander.

Steve and Old Peculier realized what this meant. As soon as they did realize, Skylord Lysander let himself go from holding onto the bridge. He plummeted down, and down, but Steve and Old Peculier could not bear to watch the rest of it. They averted their eyes, and decided to make a jump.

Fortunately, the jump succeeded and they got across safely. At first, they thought they had not a single chance to be able to jump across, but now they managed it. It was a great feat of energy that allowed them to make it.

For only a moment were their thoughts turned to happiness, and then to their deceased friend.

"We need to go down there, and get him. Even if it is just a bit of his hat, or a bit of his backpack, we need something to remember him by." replied Old Peculier, as he started walking along a rough path down to the lava pit. As he walked, bits of loose netherack gravel tumbled down with him.

"I agree, let's go. We need something." agreed Steve, as he followed close behind Old Peculier.

It was a fairly long path, and they passed a little group of zombie pig men, and they saw a Ghast, but the Ghast didn't see them. It was odd, because out in the open, there was not an enemy to be seen. But in the hidden and whenever the try to be stealthy, they end up finding lots of them!

"Here we are." Said Old Peculier glumly.

"Wait a minute… I don't think he is dead!" exclaimed Steve in happiness.

"Yes! There he is!"

Skylord Lysander was sat there, crouched underneath a little netherack overhang. They walked over to him, and started talking to him.

"Hello, Skylord Lysander!" said Old Peculier happily.

"You found me, didn't you." Replied Skylord Lysander, who had his back turned.

"Yes, we did."

"Oh well, it was worth a try." As Skylord Lysander said this, he turned around to face them both. "Why did you come down here?"

"We wanted a thing to remember you by, like a bit of armor, or a sword." Replied Old Peculier.

"Oh, yes, you would, wouldn't you." Replied Skylord Lysander, who, on revision, actually felt quite silly.

"Why did you hide?" asked Steve, as he picked a few netherack chips off his shoes.

"Oh, I didn't mean to. The sword slid from my holster, and stabbed into the side of the wall, while going down. But it was still lodged in my holster, so it suspended me in mid air. After I realized I wasn't dead, I used my sword and my shoes to carefully climb down. And I wasn't hiding, I was trying to iron out a dent in my sword. Only when I heard you coming did I start hiding, just for fun."

"Oh… I see." Replied Old Peculier. "Don't you think it was a bit mean to hide?"

"It was only meant as some fun, not to hurt anyone, and it didn't, did it?" he asked.

"Well, no, I suppose not."

"See? Just fun."

"So let us go and fight for the freedom of Notch, yes? Who is with me?" said Steve, as he started backing towards the path they had just come from.

"I am with you!" exclaimed Old Peculier.

"I am with you, as well!" exclaimed Skylord Lysander, almost simultaneous to Old Peculier.

"Then let's go!"

As Steve said that, they all took off, trudging up the small path.

When they got back up to the top, they looked around.

"Which way did we come from, again?" asked Old Peculier, as he looked in two directions.

"Um, the one with the giant break in it. Or hole, if you like." Replied Skylord Lysander, as he too looked. However, he actually found the one with the hole. "Oh, that one! So we go in this direction." As Skylord Lysander said this, he pointed to the giant gap, and then the direction they actually should go in.

"Okay, then. Let's go." Replied Old Peculier, as he followed Skylord Lysander.

"Time does tick, we need to proceed with much haste." Replied Skylord Lysander.

"I agree. Come on!"

Steve ran ahead to the front of the group, and started telling them to hurry up, or else Notch would get killed by Herobrine.

"Do you want Notch to die at the hand work of Herobrine? Walk with haste! We don't have much time to spare!"

They walked for quite a while again, and they still saw no zombie pig men, or Ghasts, or any sort of enemy. However, what did stop them, was a large castle.

"Oh my god, what is that?" asked Old Peculier, as he slowly inched his way to the position behind Skylord Lysander.

"Mr. Georgius, I believe that is a castle of Herobrine's making. I do not think of it as wise to enter. However, if we could destroy it, then that would renew this area to Notch's kingdom."

Replied Skylord Lysander. He stepped forward a bit, to get a closer look at something through the window.

"We could make this a part of Notch's kingdom?" asked Steve, who was puzzled over how that would work.

"Yes, that is how the law works. As long as we state ourselves as warriors of Notch, then if we win, Notch will gain control. And judging by the size of it, it could rule a fair way. About a half mile radius, more or less."

"That sounds like a useful advantage point, as Notch currently has no power over the land of Minecraftia. But how would he know that he rules it now?" asked Old Peculier.

"He knows, he can sense it. He will send dead people, who have waited in his place down to man these castles. And they will be gifted certain potion making abilities, such as being able to make potions of strength, or of speed, or of enchantment. Either way, it will turn out better for them. Anyway, are we ready?" asked Skylord Lysander as he drew his sword. However, his question soon became unnecessary, and completely inapplicable to anything he had just said. This was because instead of everyone shouting that they were ready and running up to the castle, the enemies in the castle already noticed them, when Skylord Lysander drew his sword. The sword glowed brightly, due to the nature of the sword, and threw light into the windows of the castle.

"Raktark, maboon!" shouted a harsh voice from the inside of the castle.

"What was that?" asked Steve, with a slight quiver in his voice.

"I think it was the ancient language of Herobrine. It is only spoken…" Skylord Lysander trailed off, and looked at the castle, with two expressions. Fear, and the sort of 'what?' feeling you get, when someone says something like 'I found your keys in my old pair of shoes.'.

"Is only spoken… what?" asked Steve, as some of Skylord Lysander's fear started to rub off on to Steve.

"It is only spoken when Herobrine is around, and it is only spoken by Herobrine as a full time language. And that means that Herobrine is right in that castle. And we can't run, we can't hide, we can only try to fight him. It is hopeless."

"Well, isn't that nice? 'It is hopeless'. Thanks, that boosts my morale a lot." Snapped Old Peculier.

"Noko ma tempo! Gartan yoo! Gartan yoo!" shouted that same coarse voice. It sounded dry, and it reminded Steve of the time he saw the Nazgúl on Lord of the Rings. The voice had a sort of shrieking overtone to it, there were thin screams coming whenever it spoke.

"Noko... does that mean no?" asked Steve. As he said 'noko' he felt a freezing cold shiver in his mind, and then it ran down his spine. It lingered for a moment, and then it seemed to disperse throughout his body.

"Sh! Don't say that! It could corrupt you!" warned Skylord Lysander, as he put his hand over Steve's mouth. "In answer to your question, I am guessing that you are correct, it does mean no."

"Okay, but the rest of it? Would that mean time? If it does, that would mean that they are saying 'no time', or 'not time'. And that means that they are leaving? I really hope so."

"Yo letré por zerth!" shouted the same voice. Within about a second, a large flash of dark purple light erupted, and shot quickly dispersing smoke into the air.

"Um, what does that mean?" asked Steve, as something broke the castle door, and about 5 or 6 Ghasts came through the breach, accompanied by an army of zombie pig men.

"I think it means 'charge' or something like that." Said Old Peculier, as he drew his sword.

"Yeah... either way, there are a ton of enemies coming for us, about to eat our heads. While we are alive." Replied Steve, as he lifted his sword over his head, as a Ghast's fireball came perilously close. The fireball hit into the sword, and bounced back again, towards a group of zombie pig men. The fireball hit the center of the group, and sent a number of zombie pig men getting thrown against the wall.

Skylord Lysander held his sword up, and shouted a few words. "Markulicus, bathemei!". And as he said that, his sword glowed much brighter, and seemed to blind about 2 of the Ghasts. The blinded Ghasts spun around in circles for a minute, and then crashed into the army of zombie pig men.

Soon, a lot of the army was destroyed, and in ruins. All the Ghasts were dead, and there were only a few zombie pig men, who somehow escaped the destruction that Steve, Old Peculier, and most of all, Skylord Lysander had caused.

"Oh yeah. Is that all of them?" asked Steve, who was half celebrating defeating a whole army, and half worried for what lingers inside.

"As far as we know, that is only the main army. There are still enemies inside, probably. We need to keep it safe, while Notch begins the transfer to send down troops." Replied Skylord Lysander, as he stepped forward cautiously

"Okay then, let's go! We need to get inside, yes? I think we should go inside the castle, take out any enemies that are left behind, and then protect it until we have the castle back." Recommended Steve, as he followed Skylord Lysander into the building.

When they entered, there was no body else there. There were only a left over of what looked like the same slippery cartilage that they were supposed to eat in the jail cell. Apart from that, there was no other type of enemy, friend, interesting thing to point out, or even a different tone in the dark red-purple of the wall. There was only countless stairways, doors to identical rooms, and corridors. They thought that it was true that every single room was identical, until they found this room.

The only different room they found, had an altar, and it had a large pool of water in it. It had an unfriendly purple glow to it, and the glow was coming from a purple crystal, plugged into a slot.

"Hm, maybe if we put the crystals that we have into that, it will activate the altar, and allow Notch's men to come down here a lot quicker." Said Old Peculier, who was completely guessing about what they should do next.

"Wait, you have crystals? It will only work if the crystals are uninfected obsidian, otherwise it will just summon more of the enemies." Said Skylord Lysander, who did not know for an instant that the had crystals. He looked at Old Peculier with very wide eyes.

"Yes, and mine is uninfected. I could just take out this one and put in this little chip of obsidian, then?" asked Old Peculier.

"Yes, that should be the only thing you need to do. And then, with any luck, a lot of Notch's men shall spawn in the water, and then the castle will be ruled by Notch!"

"Good, I don't want a great big hassle just because I can't take the crystal out, or something."

With that, Old Peculier carefully removed the dark purple crystal from the center, and put in a darker purple crystal in. As soon as he did that, he noticed a glow from the ceiling.

"Presumably they are the men who will protect the castle?" asked Old Peculier, who was not taking his eyes off the nice sight of seeing people materialize in a bright glow.

"I think so, but they won't come immediately. Notch right not is *creating matter*, which is incredibly hard to do without breaking physics completely." Replied Skylord Lysander, as he peeled his eyes away, only to catch a much worse sight. "Quick! Over there! I see more of Herobrines troops coming to destroy us! They do not want Notch to gain a foothold here, under any circumstances. This is Herobrine's main base to get to the Over world, if Notch takes it, then they will have to find another way in!"

They could here the completely uniform marching of the zombie pig men, and the moans of the Ghasts.

"Not good." Muttered Steve, as he drew his sword. "Skylord Lysander! Take out your sword!"

"Yes, I shall need it." Replied Skylord Lysander, as he drew his sword, and again, his sword glowed very brightly.

Skylord Lysander ran to the front of the party, and stood there, readily at the door of the room where they were all standing and watching. Steve joined Skylord Lysander, and stood behind him.

"Old Peculier! Come and fight with us!" called Steve, who could hear the marching of the army near the door.

"Um, Old Peculier, you shouldn't do that! We need a port to concentrate the energy into the spawn pool. If you fight, you couldn't be the port. Keep concentrating!" warned Skylord Lysander, who only just took his eyes off the door for a second, and then resumed looking at the door, as he noticed they could only be about a couple of feet or so away.

"Get ready to fight, Skylord Lys-" before Steve could finish the sentence, a hoard of zombie pig men broke through the door, and started snarling and running as if they were rabid. Steve had never seen them quite as agitated and wild as this.

"These zombie pig men have a stage 4 virus, the highest and final stage of their zombie lifespan. They only have twenty, maybe twenty five minutes until the zombie virus has absorbed all the minerals and vitamins in their body, and tries to make itself as contagious as possible."

Soon, those zombie pig men were attacking them. They started bearing their teeth, and clawing their way through each other to kill Steve and Skylord Lysander. Skylord Lysander struck a very effective blow against them, that caused many heads of the zombie pig men to be cut off, and rolled around on the floor. And one of those heads, quite comically tripped another zombie pig man and he got trampled.

"We need to kill them faster!" shouted Skylord Lysander over the din of many zombie pig men snarling and growling, and in some cases screaming in frustration.

"I know! I am going as fast as I can! I hate these god forsaken mindless zombies, and I hate this whole god forsaken 'Nether' place!" shouted Steve to Skylord Lysander.

Suddenly, a small group of zombie pig men dropped to the ground and started convulsing.

"I think they reached their life span limit!" shouted Skylord Lysander, as he glided his sword through another pack of them.

"I-" said a very buzzed out sort of voice, that got cut off. "I-(fizzle) he-(fizzle) ord-(fizzle) Notch-(fizzle)."

"I think that the troops from Notch's army are starting to get here very quickly, as I can see them weave together before my very eyes!" said Old Peculier, as he moved away from the battle between the zombie pig men, and Steve and Skylord Lysander.

"You he-(fizzle) me?" asked the voice, that seemed to be coming from the person in the spawning pool.

"Almost! Just wait a minute! You are still spawning in!" shouted Old Peculier, as the person's facial features were just barely visible.

"You here me now?" asked the voice, completely fluently, without any fizzling or buzzing.

"Yes! What is your message?" asked Old Peculier, as he bent over the large crystal holder just in front of the spawning pool.

"I am here on the order of Notch, we are not invaders." Said the voice once again.

"Yes, we know that. Although currently we have a slight problem with the zombie pig men, and there are Ghasts right outside." Replied Old Peculier, as a few more people appeared.

"I see, I brought a sword. I should be able to help them."

"Yes! By all means, we really could use some! We are getting pushed back!" shouted Skylord Lysander, as he brought another load of zombie pig men to the ground.

"Just a few seconds, I am still spawning!" shouted the person back to him. After about five or ten seconds, the person jumped out of the spawning pool, and pulled out a very bright, glowing sword from his holster. "I am an advanced fighter, a Skylord. I have heard that there are not many Skylords left in Minecraftia, so I am glad to be brought back to the lands!"

"I am also a Skylord!" said Skylord Lysander, as he compared his glowing sword to the other Skylord's.

"Ah, very good. We shall have these enemies pushed back in no time! My name is Skylord Hurtmull. Nice to meet you, what is your name, Skylord?" asked the person who is now apparent to be Skylord Hurtmull.

"My name is Skylord Lysander. Now let's kill these foul troops of Herobrine!" replied Skylord Lysander, as he turned away from Skylord Hurtmull.

"I agree!"

By the time that they had finished their brief exchange, the rest of the people had appeared.

"Hello! Who are you two? I know who you are, Skylord Hurtmull, but who are your friends?" asked the person, just randomly and casually as if they were not in a battle to protect the well ship of Minecraftia.

"I am Skylord Lysander, and this is Steve." Replied Skylord Lysander quickly.

"Hello!" said Steve as he waved to the person with his free hand.

"Now could you help us? There are spare swords over there, if you want them! I hope you brought your own, because those are rusted and tattered. Hurry up! We can not hold off there zombie pig men forever, you know!"

"Yes, and yes, I brought my own sword. Just in case you didn't have any spare. Men, to battle!" replied the person, as he ordered 5 people to draw a sword and start hacking apart the forces of Herobrine, and he joined them.

After about 2 minutes of brutal fighting, the last Ghasts disappeared from sight.

"That took care of the problem!" exclaimed Steve, as he leant against the doorway to the other rooms, as he watched the last few Ghasts leave.

"I agree. So, can you guys take care of this castle?" asked Old Peculier.

"Yes, I believe so. If we can't then Notch will send down a few more troops for us. He will also periodically send us someth ing to eat, I mean, it isn't going to be nice, because the molecules get jumbled up when sending down non-sentient things."

"I see. Well, are we ready to go?" asked Old Peculier, as he started walking towards the door.

"I think so. Let's go!" replied Skylord Lysander, as he checked through his stuff.

"I am well packed, just need to go for me, as well!" exclaimed Steve.

"What do you mean, 'just need to go for me'?" asked Skylord Lysander.

"Like, just need to go to be ready."

"Oh, sorry. I didn't know what you meant."

"Anyway, let's go."

Skylord Lysander, followed by Steve, and then followed by Old Peculier left the building, and started walking in the direction that a path was leading.

"So, Skylord Lysander, how do you become a Skylord?" asked Steve, as he looked at the fine artwork on the holder for Skylord Lysander's sword.

"Well, first, you need to go to the land of Skylords, and then you need to go to the trainer. You will have to train for about five, six, or maybe even ten years, and then you should gain your sword, marked with the certificate that allows you to be a Skylord. So, in a way, your sword is your certificate." Replied Skylord Lysander, as he pulled his sword out from it's holder about half way, and inspected the markings. "You also get to have the word 'Skylord' in front of your name at all times, whether it is on a form, or on a city citizen count. It is made illegal to punish someone for making someone put down their name without the prefix of 'Skylord'. If they are a Skylord, then they are allowed to put it in front of their name, or to not. It depends if they want to or not."

"I see, so, presumably the land of Skylords is in the Over world, not the Nether, yes?" asked Steve.

"Yes, it is in the Over world. And even if we were in the Over world, I am **not** taking you there again under any circumstances. It is too insecure. At any given time, the forces of Herobrine could just decide to land in there, and take over."

"Well, I suppose it would be annoying to spend up to ten years there, anyway." Said Steve, who was trying to justify not being able to go there. Nor did he really want to go, considering the security. There were no doors to houses, and there were not roofs to certain buildings holding priceless artifacts.

They walked the rest of the way in silence. When they finally got to the next landmark, they noticed that it was not a castle, by far. It was a small tribal village.

"What is that? Do you know of that village?" asked Old Peculier.

"No, probably a small camp for Herobrine's forces." Replied Skylord Lysander.

"Yeah, I think so as well. That seems to be the only thing that is in the Nether." Replied Steve.

Steve, Old Peculier and Skylord Lysander all walked towards the village.

"Welcome (oink) to our village! (oink)" said a voice, that was coming from right next to them. But when they turned around, they saw that there was not a man there, like they expected, but instead an uninfected pig man. "Hello? (oink)"

"Yes, hello, how are you not infected with the zombie virus that has been passed around your kind?" asked Steve, as he looked at that pig man with awe of not only that he was a walking and talking pig, but also that he was not a brain dead, zombie, gargling pig man.

"Not all of us are infected, in fact, around fifty percent of the population of pig men are not zombies. The survivors built small camps around the Nether, for protection, and a place to live. It isn't easy, but we can make it, just about." Replied the pig man, who had no snout, unlike other pigs.

"I see, but, how do you keep yourself uninfected? And where do you hide? And why isn't your style of life fine?" asked Old Peculier in disbelief.

"We keep ourselves away from any zombie pig men, and also keep away from any sign of rotting, any sign of enemies coming from anywhere. And as for hiding, we don't *hide* as such, we just move our city every once in a while. We push the houses, and most of the time the houses will stay intact, and not break. And as for not too good style of life, well, we are living in a fiery place with no animals or soil to kill or harvest or grow, and we need to move every so often, just to keep us from being noticed. And also, there is a marauding zombie virus on the loose that will kill anyone who gets infected with it. A bit stressful, if you ask me." Replied the pig man.

"Wait, you were going 'oink' in the first sentence you said to us, why not now?" asked Steve.

"Oh, I was just clearing my throat. I can't talk very well without a clear throat."

"Well, to be honest, that sounds like a very big cliché…" noted Old Peculier.

"I *am* a humanoid pig, cut me some slack."

"Okay then."

"Why do you think that you are less then other people?" asked Steve.

"Because I once was a normal person, but then I got into a Nether portal, but at the same time, a pig went through the portal with me. I thought at first that the Nether portal on the other side had deactivated before I got to it, but I realized that my hands were pink, and the pink was spreading to other parts of my body, such as my arms, chest, feet, legs, and I also seemed to not be able to think as clearly, for example, I just can't do mathematics, or judge distances, or even put clothes on. I can only talk normally, walk around and push things. My eyesight has been extremely badly damaged, I now can only see things through a dark haze. Apparently some people had it better, the children of my race, and the other people who also got a bit of the pig's DNA mixed into their own DNA. Some of them can even do difficult sciences, like physics. I had it quite badly, considering my eyesight *and* my thoughts are damaged. Although when you went through them portal, you didn't get mutated. You ought to be very, very grateful."

"I am very grateful, I need my eyesight and clear thought to attack enemies well, and to do anything else, really." Replied Steve.

"I second that emotion." Replied Old Peculier.

"Well, no use just standing there. You adventurers, go and free us from Herobrine!" said the pig man, as he ushered them away, but politely.

"We have already moved you into Notch's kingdom. We captured a castle, and now Notch will be ruling a large portion of the Nether. And, in fact, here comes the terraforming." Stated Skylord Lysander.

"Terraforming? What terraforming?" asked the pig man, as he looked around frantically.

"That… terraforming…" said Steve very slowly, as he watched the spectacle of the Nether's materials, like glowstone, soul sand and netherack getting changed into trees, grass, sand, stone, dirt, clay and ocean. The oceans that seemed to unfold from a certain point, but Steve could never pin point that exact place, filled the lava filled valleys, and turned them into obsidian that then got layered with the oncoming water.

"Wow, why is that happening?" asked the pig man.

"As I said, because we captured some land for Notch, so he is making this land his own, instead of Herobrine's." replied Skylord Lysander, as he tried as hard as he could to see where the water was coming from.

"Oh, yeah. I forgot."

"KARATAKA MU'U!" shouted an annoyed, rough and commanding voice.

"MUF L'AH GRAKNOR!" replied another voice.

"MU TIGO!"

"What is that?" asked Old Peculier, as he started to panic a bit more, because he felt he just could not take another battle against Herobrine's soldiers, in the Nether, while he is barely awake.

"I think that would be Herobrine's soldiers getting mighty annoyed because their precious Nether resources are being taken and changed into Over world resources, and there is water everywhere that is destroying their odds of winning, troops and bases." Replied Skylord Lysander, as he was not taking his eyes off it, even to blink. Because of this, his eyes burned with searing pain, that could be easily waved away just by blinking, but the sight was so nice, that he dared not blink in case of missing a single second of it.

"Yep, I guessed. But, doesn't this mean that now the Nether and Herobrine are aware of our presence, and will do anything to stop us? Because it sure feels that way, with all the fact about yelling angry people, and the fact we are ruining important places that are bases for Herobrine, and now they are going to be offering expensive bounties for our heads? I think that that might be an issue." Exclaimed Steve, as he managed to take his eyes off of it, just because it was slowing, and most of the camps that were near the shore were gone, washed away with the flow of the water.

"Yeah, a bit of a down side, I suppose. But we will have more of Notch's troops coming to assist us. So it balances out. Only problem is, is that it will be quite difficult for us to keep a low profile, because they will always have troops looking for us, and Herobrine's troops are monsters, they never need to sleep, rest or eat. The only thing they need is the will of Herobrine to allow them to live. Otherwise, they would just fall apart, and be nothing. His troops are nothing more than a weaker proxy of his will. As long as he controls them, they will still live. Just like puppets, they will live while the string holder is holding the strings, but if the string holder were to let go, the puppet falls limp." Said Skylord Lysander, as he, also took his eyes away from the flooding. He was running his fingers down his sword holder while he was saying this, occasionally looking at the foreign writing on it.

"I see, so, couldn't we just go to the next castle and knock that one down as well?" asked Steve, who was not seeing the point of the Skylord's massive explanation.

"No, we can't. I heard the calls, those, in a nutshell, mean that they are going to summon Ender Dragons. Do you remember the Ender Dragon that you fought back in the Over world? That one was weakened. It had small pads, attached to certain parts of the body, that were being electrocuted, that zapped the brains of the Ender Dragons. It caused muscle spasms, and it was tame!" exclaimed Skylord Lysander.

"How did you know about the Ender Dragon we fought?" asked Steve, who narrowed his eyes at Skylord Lysander.

"That Ender Dragon, the one that you fought and almost killed? Sending it barely flying off? That one was a tame one. It was the first Ender Dragon to be tamed. It had only been tamed for about two years, and it takes a little over two thousand five hundred years to tame it! But then someone captured it, and made people fight against it. When it flew off, it went back to it's original owner, who then notified me about someone who was mistreating it. But, before I could make sure that person was brought to justice, or even before I could leave the city, I got trapped by Herobrine. And then you came and freed us all!" explained Skylord Lysander, who had a barely angry tone in his voice.

"Why would he capture the first tame Ender Dragon?" asked Steve.

"Well, I don't know. Maybe for the fame, the fortune, or maybe just so that he could annoy people. But I can tell you one thing, it probably is not for a good, nice reason. Like most of them, I bet it is just for bad things." Replied Skylord Lysander.

"Where can you even find wild Ender Dragons? Where do you get them from to be tamed in the first place?"

"That would be The End, the dimension that you can not come out of without having to kill Herobrine, and then Notch will come down from his land and allow you to have anything, and go anywhere, and then Notch shall rule everything, and Herobrine will be defeated. But, one does not simply walk into The End. You need at least somebody to help you fight, and two people will not do. You need about two thousand to deal with all the Endermen, the Ender Dragons, and then Herobrine. Without an army, you will be ripped to shreds instantly." Replied Skylord Lysander.

"And where could we get such a large army?"

"Well, we could get an army if we first capture the Nether, and then we could summon Notch to speak with us, and we could ask him if it is time to send his army down to The End. If he replies with the positive, then we go to an ancient strong hold, built by the ancient other faction, called the Earthlords. They were the only people who could access The End, but it soon hit them right back. Soon, they had established portals in there, and Herobrine was sending false signals to the Earthlords, and so the rest of the Earthlords think that The End is safe, but anyone who enters will die. Eventually, Herobrine escapes from The End, and enters the Nether, and the Over world. Anyway, if we go to one of the strong holds, then we could use one of the End portals, and get to the End. Unfortunately, when the Earthlords realized that The End was dangerous and letting Herobrine into the other worlds, then they took most of the keys out of it. The keys, being eyes of Endermen. Very rare, but now we can create them just by collecting the Ender pearl in the middle of and Enderman's otherwise obsidian coating, and mixing it with a blaze rod."

"But where would we get a blaze rod?"

"From some of Herobrine's troops, only found in very important Nether castles. If you kill them, you can take the blaze rods that will fall limp around their body, that would normally be orbiting the golem like planets around a sun that wants to kill you."

"Okay, so it is not going to be easy. So what do we do now?" asked Steve.

"I suggest that we continue to go to some of the less important castles. There are less likely chances that Herobrine will have an Ender Dragon there, because they are rare, and very dangerous."

"That one looks quite, um, fairly, um, not advanced?" said Steve, as he pointed to a primitive castle. Well, primitive compared to the rest. The reason that he said 'um' was probably because the phrase 'fairly not advanced' does not make any sense.

"Yes, I agree. We shall go there, next, and hope nothing bad happens. Wait a minute… what is that sound?" asked Skylord Lysander, as he strained to hear a loud flapping sound. Suddenly, something quite close let out an ear breaking roar.

"Is that an Ender Dragon?" asked Old Peculier, as he started to slowly draw his sword.

"Yes, I believe it is." Muttered Skylord Lysander, as he just caught sight of it. There was someone –or something- riding on it's back. The dragon was completely pitch black, and had purple eyes, emitting small particles, that looked like smoke. It had no visible teeth, but that was not to say it is not a very painful way to die if you are caught underneath it's mighty, heavy jaws. At the end of it's very long wings, it had sharp claws, that were twitching, as if it really wanted to scratch something.

"YAKIRAR MUR!" shouted the person on the Ender Dragon, as it kicked the Ender Dragon and pointed to Steve, Old Peculier, and Skylord Lysander.

"Now, it is time to run. I think he is sending the Ender Dragon to come and kill us. Now, run! RUN!" shouted Skylord Lysander, as he started to run towards the ocean that had newly formed.

"Running! Come on, Old Peculier!" shouted Steve as he closely followed Skylord Lysander. Soon, Old Peculier started following Steve and Skylord Lysander, to the ocean.

"DU'UTH YUGRAM!" bellowed the Ender Dragon, as lots of purple energy shot from it's mouth, and struck one of Notch's trees.

"It is trying to destroy Notch's kingdom!" shouted Steve, as he looked at the burning tree, that set fire to small portions of grass.

"I know! We can only run into the ocean, where we will be safe! There is no chance that we can destroy an Ender Dragon! Keep running!" shouted Skylord Lysander.

"And I certainly don't want to try!" shouted Old Peculier, as he started running out of breath.

"Wise decision!" replied Skylord Lysander, as he was about ten, maybe fifteen meters away from the ocean. "Almost there!"

"Hurry!" shouted Steve.

"AGRATU! AGRATU!" shouted the person on the Ender Dragon. Suddenly, the Ender Dragon swerved towards Steve, Old Peculier, and Skylord Lysander.

"It is coming towards us! We need to speed up!" shouted Old Peculier, as he used his last burst of energy to run towards the ocean. Skylord Lysander had already jumped into the ocean, and had dove under the surface of the water.

"Skylord Lysander! Come above the surface! You will drown!" shouted Steve, as he also went into the water. When he heard no reply, he dove underneath the surface as well, and went to retrieve Skylord Lysander. But, strangely, he did not feel like the medium outside his body was unusual, or even something that he could not breath.

"It is okay, Mr. Persson. When I entered the Nether portal, then we all got mutated, and we are a very small portion dead. We do not need to breath for a short amount of time, because I had cast and enchantment around us, that allows us to breathe underwater. And because we are already slightly dead, that makes it easier to cast the spell. Don't worry." Explained Skylord Lysander, as Steve started to breathe underwater. At first, he let out a large cough, and exhaled all the air in his lungs. Then, he very slowly and hardly inhaled the much heavier water.

"I see, thank you for casting the enchantment. It will help, because I don't want to drown underwater, or to be eaten alive by an Ender Dragon. But can't the Ender Dragon just look under the horizon of the water? It is transparent!" exclaimed Steve, as he looked up at the Ender Dragon flying overhead.

"No, the way that it's vision works, it can't see anything underwater, instead it's brain doesn't know what to make of water, so it just thinks it is End Stone, the type of stone that it's home realm is made out of. To the Ender Dragon, we just jumped inside a load of End Stone, and probably suffocated." replied Skylord Lysander.

"Hah, funny. Obviously isn't too bright, if it thinks we can jump through a type of stone!" joked Steve. "Actually, you do know a lot about these things, how do you know so much?"

"Oh, a lot of sources, some of them are through books on these matters, and most bits of information that I get are from my training as a Skylord. A lot of Skylords also get the training as an Earthlord, and a Flamelord. This is because the Earthlords and Flamelords both have been destroyed by Herobrine's forces, and there is no other person to hold their knowledge, so it is passed down the ancestry chain of Skylords."

"But what is the difference between Skylords, Earthlords and Flamelords?" asked Steve.

"Well, Skylords are masters of the sky, and will normally establish bases, on airships, or just really tall buildings. Earthlords will live in caves underground, or make their own large holes. Flamelords normally live in deserts, where it is very hot. They make large buildings, with open roofs that have fire altars in the center. There are also Waterlords, who make their bases underwater. They are very intelligent, and provide the other elemental lords with good technology. They enchanted my sword for me, and that is why it glows."

Through out this conversation, Old Peculier had been just standing behind them. The Ender Dragon let out a final roar, and returned to a castle.

"I think it is gone." Said Old Peculier, as he started to carefully return to the surface.

"Oh! Mr. Georgius! I did not notice your presence." Exclaimed Skylord Lysander as he started floating to the surface. "Anyway, yes. I think that it would be gone, after all, it *is* actually leaving as we speak. I think that means it is gone." Skylord Lysander sounded a bit sarcastic while saying that.

"Are you sure?" asked Steve, as he very cautiously floated up to the surface, just barely poking his eyes over the surface to see if the Ender Dragon was still searching for them.

"Yes, it has landed in a castle. That is the good thing, the bad thing is that that was the Ender Dragon just landed in the castle we were going to invade." Said Skylord Lysander, as he started walking out of the ocean.

"So now we have no chance of entering the castle, yes?" asked Steve, as he followed Skylord Lysander out of the water, and Old Peculier was very close behind.

"Yeah, not good. Very bad. So now we need to do other things. What do you suggest that we do now?" asked Skylord Lysander, who felt quite hopeless.

"I suggest that we go to the Over world, and go and find someone who can help us." Replied Old Peculier, as he looked around, for any signs of a portal that could take them back to their (Except for Steve's) home land.

"Yes, sounds feasible. But where could we find a Over world portal here?" asked Steve, as he joined in looking.

"I don't know. Maybe in the castle that we destroyed Herobrine's forces and established a base for Notch? They would need a portal to get resources back and forth between the castle and the Over world, right?" asked Old Peculier.

"Yes, I suppose so. But they said that Notch was going to send them food periodically, so they might not have built it."

"But they also said it would not taste very nice, so maybe they wanted a portal to get more food from chickens, steak from cows, and pork from pigs. I say we just go there to find out."

"I agree. Let's go!" exclaimed Skylord Lysander, as he started to walk towards the castle they had newly freed up.

"Are you sure about walking into the open? I mean, there are people who are following us for a fairly large bounty, it is not really very safe for us just to walk over there. If anything, we should run over there, or jog to make sure that we do not gather any unwanted attention." Suggested Steve, as he grabbed onto Skylord Lysander's arm.

"Yes, good idea. I say that we should jog there. Let us go!" replied Skylord Lysander more quietly then he had previously said things.

# Chapter 22

After a lot of jogging, they finally got to the gates of the castle. They stopped jogging, and knocked on the flimsy, rebuilt door.

"Name? Intentions?" called a voice, that sounded like Skylord Jasper.

"My name is Skylord Lysander, and I am with two friends, Steve and Old Peculier. My intentions are to use your portal to get back to the Over world! I need to be allowed in." replied Skylord Lysander, as he introduces Steve and Old Peculier, but he suspected he would not need to really introduce them.

"Ah, Skylord Lysander! Come in. I have much to tell you about what our stay at the castle has been like." Replied the voice, as they heard the grating of the latch rub against the iron door. Soon, the iron door swung open, and Skylord Jasper was standing there.

"Skylord Jasper, how have you been?" asked Steve.

"Well, first of all there have not been any more attacks from Herobrine, so it has been a bit boring. Not that I am complaining, though, because I don't particularly want enemies bursting the doors down every few minutes. How ever, I did see a rather nasty looking Ender Dragon, and it seemed that the rider saw something, and it might have taken a picture of it, and that thing it was looking at was probably you three. Just a heads up to let you know that they probably have a picture of you stored, so they can recognize you. Just be careful about going places, because they will see you, compare you to the records that they held, and then slaughter you without a second thought." Replied Skylord Jasper, welcomingly, but then it became not so welcoming when he started talking about the fact that Herobrine probably has a fairly heavy bounty on Steve, Skylord Lysander and Old Peculier.

"Yes, lovely, we are going to be exclusively hunted out, we know. Now can we please use the portal? We need to hurry, because of the fact that people are searching for us all over the place." Said Steve very quickly.

"Actually, no."

"What did you say?" asked Old Peculier in disbelief.

"I said no. You may NOT use my portal."

"Why?"

"Herobrine gives good rewards for that bounty."

"You can't be serious! You didn't, did you?" asked Skylord Lysander, as he started looking for the easiest exit. The iron door had locked behind them, and there was only a small hole on the wall he might be able to fit through.

"Oh yes, I did. In fact, I brought some little helpers." Replied Skylord Jasper, as he gestured for something to come out of a very dark, sinister shadow.

Immediately after he made the gesture, about three Endermen crawled out of the little dark hole, unfurling from hunched positions. Steve, Old Peculier and Skylord Lysander would recognize those spidery limbs anywhere.

"Endermen! Jasper, how could you?" asked Skylord Lysander, who deliberately called him just 'Jasper' instead of 'Skylord Jasper'.

"That is SKYLORD Jasper, thank you very much. And yes, they are Endermen. My elite soldiers."

"Don't get... ahead of your... yourself there... Jasper!" warned one of the Endermen.

"Oh, all right! But remember, for this mission, I am your commander."

"Yes sir."

"That is not Skylord Jasper anymore. By the power I have received from Notch, I here by revoke your Skylord properties, and title." Said Skylord Lysander bravely.

"YOU TAKE THAT BACK!" spat Jasper fiercely.

"No, I can not have a corrupt Skylord roam Minecraftia."

"Endermen, grab hold of him!"

The Endermen did as they were told immediately. They ran over to the last Skylord in the room, and grabbed his arms, and threw him to the wall.

"Take it back, or my Endermen will kill you."

"Never! I will never take it back, even if you kill me!" shouted Skylord Lysander.

"Your loss, then. Guards, begin operation 2-8a." After that, the Endermen relaxed their hold on him, and started concentrating a purple light from their chest.

"Jasper, you don't know what you are doing! Stop this! IT WON'T JUST DESTROY ME!" screamed Skylord Lysander, as he could only stare in wild fright at their chest.

"Who cares? You are going to either die, or you will make me a Skylord again. I will give you three seconds."

"Jasper, no!"

"3..."

"Jasper, please!" shouted Steve, who had just been watching in morbid shock until now.

"2..."

"JASPER!"

"1… Are you sure you don't want to?"

"Never!"

"ZERO! Time up! Endermen, finish him."

"JASPEEERRR!"

Within seconds, the beam in the middle of the Endermen's chests erupted, and very quickly it struck Skylord Lysander. At first, nothing happened for a few seconds. And then, Skylord Lysander's body collected a purple and green ball of energy around it. After a few seconds he managed to struggle one word out of himself.

"Run…" he croaked.

After a second or so of hearing Skylord Lysander's command, Steve and Old Peculier burst into movement. Steve managed to use his shoulder to burst out of the iron door, and Old Peculier threw the broken latch at one of the Endermen, but he did not stick around long enough to see if it hit.

Soon, they noticed that the whole castle was collecting purple and green energy. The ball of it grew bigger and bigger, until they could hear the snaps and crackles of it from a mile away. They couldn't really here anything over the din. It got louder, Steve and Old Peculier ran faster and further, until the energy around it all dispersed very quickly. It exploded, causing the castle walls to fly in all directions. There was the iron door they had burst through flying overhead, and what looked to be an Ender pearl from the center of an Enderman that collided with the door, sending both pieces of shrapnel flying apart.

"Look at that!" shouted Steve, as he pointed behind him, to a wave of either sound, or some sort of shockwave.

"Oh no…" muttered Old Peculier, as he looked. He turned around, slowed and just stood there in helpless fascination of the shockwave.

"Old Peculier!" shouted Steve, as the cloud of dust, bricks and other pieces of shrapnel engulfed Old Peculier as well.

Steve kept running, but it was no use. He ran, and ran, but eventually the shockwave engulfed him, just like Old Peculier had disappeared amidst dust and stone.


End of Part 3


Part 4
Untimely Incidents

# Chapter 23

Steve woke up slowly. He was on a bed, which he definitely did not expect.

"Ah, you are awake. Finally." Came a voice. Steve slowly realized it was coming from the person standing just to the left of him. "In case you are wondering, I am the doctor here. You seem to have some minor head trauma, but it is clearing away quickly. You have been passed out for quite a while, for about three days. We just found you, laying there on the ground, so we brought you into the hospital of Yerta."

"Yerta? Where is that?" replied Steve, slowly and tiredly.

"It is in Minecraftia, near the North end."

"What is Minecraftia?"

"Oh, no. You seem to have some long term amnesia. You once knew all these things, but after you got knocked over, you don't remember anything. Not good..." The doctor jotted down some notes on a little red pad.

"How did you find me?" asked Steve.

"Well, your friend, who goes by the name of Old Peculier, dragged you back to the remains of the castle, and helped you through the Nether portal."

"Old Peculier? Castle? Nether? What is all this?"

"Hm, very bad amnesia… not good. Maybe if you see your friend you will remember him."

"Maybe." Replied Steve, and at that, the doctor pressed a button, and spoke clearly into it. "Would Old Peculier please report to room 4, repeat, Old Peculier to room 4." Soon, Old Peculier was walking up a small flight of stairs, and he carefully opened the door, and walked inside.

"Oh, hello Steve. You are awake, finally."

"I am sorry, sir, but I do not remember you. Who are you again?" replied Steve.

"My name is Old Peculier, I dragged you back to the hospital of Yerta, this place."

"I am sorry, doesn't ring a bell."

"Yes, he does have some major long term amnesia from the fall, so maybe his memory will just come back from living out his life, and doing familiar things." Said the doctor to Old Peculier, as he looked at some of the notes he had just taken down.

"So, when will he be able to come out of the hospital?" asked Old Peculier.

"Oh, I don't know, give it a day or two. He just needs to be made sure he doesn't have any neural blood clots, or severe brain damage, that's all."

"I see, so, should I tell people he will be out in a few days? Or should I just keep waiting until I get proper information?"

"Well, I'd say that you should keep quiet for a while, until we can be sure. My guess of him being out in a few days is only an estimate, I don't exactly know. If he goes very, very well, in the sense that he instantly recovers from amnesia and has no blood clots, no brain damage, or any other neural dysfunction, then he might be able to come out by tomorrow. However, if his amnesia does not clear up, or if he as any sort of clotting, etcetera, then he might have to stay here for ever. We just need to run a few tests, let him live here for a while, and then we will see if he is okay."

"Alright, then. I will just tell them that I do not know when he will be out, but he is in the hospital of Yerta."

"Good decision, I do not want any confusion or people expecting him to come out and a riot starting, so, yes. Just tell them that."

"Okay, doctor." As Old Peculier said this, he stepped out of the door, and Steve could hear him walking down the hallway.

"So then, Steve, how do you feel after a few minutes of being awake?"

"Well, I feel a bit drowsy. Could I have a cup of water?"

"Yes, certainly. I can only give it to you in half cups, though."

"Why?"

"Because if you spilt it onto the equipment, it would break it, or if you consumed too much at one given moment."

"Hm, yes, makes sense." Replied Steve, as he waited eagerly for the doctor to pour him a cup of water, from a cold tap.

"Here you go, Steve." Said the doctor as he handed Steve the cup of water, and Steve sipped carefully. "So, then. Who are you? I don't have any information on your back story."

"Well, I grew up in the humble town of Barth, and then I lived with my grandmother. I lived with her for a very long time, until she became the oldest living resident in... in... I don't know where my hometown was."

"Well, I have certainly never heard of 'Barth'. Sounds like a very clean city, get it? Barth? Bath? Clean?" laughed the doctor. Steve joined in with weak laughter.

"Have you really never heard of Barth?"

"No, no I haven't. Sorry, where is it again? Didn't quite catch it."

"I already said I don't know, sorry. If I did know, I would tell you."

"Well, I am sure that it is not so important that the life and death of the land of Minecraftia pivots around it, so just relax."

"Yeah, I guess you are right. But, I really want to find out."

"When I looked at your citizenship, I could not find any information about you. It says you just signed up to be a citizen in one place one day, and you magically appeared. Maybe you were born in the Higher Realms."

"What are the Higher Realms?"

"Well, I have heard it only as myth, but it is supposed to be the place that is the only escape from the cubes of this land. There are these things, called 'spheres' and the are like cubes, except they have no corners. Not a single corner or edge. It is like the face of a cube or cuboid all over. Where ever you touch on it, it is smooth. There are also things where you touch them, and they change shape! Not move, they actually bend! I would love to go there. It sounds like an amazing place."

"Well, for some reason I don't really think it is great. Probably has a lot of crime, stealing those spheres. They must be priceless, think about it, a real life, object that defies nature! There must be hundreds of people who rob places and what not per minute! Besides, who wants to live in a world where there is so much need to be careful, where if you drop a single sphere, then someone will steal it, take it, and run away with it! They must be so rich, they all must live like kings."

"Actually, there is much poverty."

"What? How?"

"Their currency, or so I have heard, is not in spheres."

"Why?"

"I don't know, presumably because it would be annoying to have to trade away such priceless and valuable things every day, to eat, to rent a room at an inn, to do anything!"

"Then what is their currency in?"

"Well, different bits of it say different things. I think the main one is yen, but I could be wrong. I have heard of dollars, which I think are smaller, and I have heard of euros. I think the euros are the biggest, the yen are the next biggest, but they are the main ones, and dollars are the smallest. I have only pieced it together from various different stories about going there, but I think I have a pretty good idea."

"Yes, maybe you are right. I don't know exactly, but it sounds very complicated."

"I agree. So then, are you feeling better after drinking that water?"

"Yes, I am a little bit. I have a bit of a head ache, though."

"Hm, might need to run a scan on that, just to make sure nothing is starting up."

"Will it be urgent?"

"Um, yes, it will. Nothing *really* to worry about, just a scan. Won't hurt a bit, it will probably be nothing, we are just checking."

"Okay, how soon?"

"Well, if you would just come with me now, we can have the scan right now. Do you think you are steady enough to walk?"

"I don't know. I think so."

"Well, Steve, I say just give it a try, and if you don't feel you can, just sit back down and I will get the scanning equipment, and bring it here."

"Okay, sounds feasible." After Steve said that, he slid out from under the sheet, and put one foot on the ground. '*so far so good*' he thought. He put another foot onto the floor, and started moving his torso towards the correct position. He slowly brought himself up to his feet, but fell back down, because he was feeling light headed.

"Are you okay, there Steve?" asked the doctor, as he approached Steve, to see if he needed help.

"Yes, just got a bit light headed. Gone now, just a one off thing." Steve tried to get up a second time. He got up, and started moving his legs back and forth, just to warm them up. He then slowly walked to the doctor.

"Okay, now can you follow me, do you think? Can you stand that long?"

"Yes, I think so. Let's go. Just don't go too quickly."

"Okay." The doctor started slowly walking to the appropriate room, checking back on Steve every two or three, or sometimes even five seconds, if the doctor thought that Steve was walking well for the moment. "Okay then, Steve. We are at the scanning room. If you could just lay down on that bed there, that would be a big help, because other wise, we would just be scanning the pillow."

"Yes, that would not be good." Replied Steve, as he laid down on the bed. The bed was firm, bordering on hard, but it was not causing excruciating pain. The bed started smoothly moving into a narrow tube, and then a bright light flickered on.

"As I said, this will not hurt a bit, just close your eyes, and wait for it to be done."

"Okay, doctor." Steve had already closed his eyes, because the light was so bright. There were some whirring sounds from the machine, and the hatch at the bottom closed, leaving him completely isolated in the room.

Suddenly, the light dimmed immediately, and another light came in, but it was not on. When the light dimmed, Steve opened his eyes to see what was going on, and he guessed that the second light was emitting ultra violet radiation or something, so he shut his eyes again, to keep them from getting exposed to it.

"Okay Steve, now we will pull you out, and discuss the results." called the doctor, from the other side. The hatch at Steve's feet slid open, and the bed started to move out of the small area.

"So, what were the results? Was everything okay?"

"Yes, yes. It is just that you appear to have a piece of metal embedded into you left arm. I suggest that you let us take that out. It must have been in there for quite a while, because the skin has healed over it. It is not very deep, and it is not a very big problem. Just let us do a minor bit of surgery."

"Okay, doctor. When will that be?"

"Well, I think in about two or three days, give or take. It depends when it is free. The surgery room is booked until tomorrow night, but at an operation of your extent we just can not operate at night."

"But I thought you said it was a minor bit of surgery, right?"

"Well, it is. But even minor surgery can not be performed at night."

"Okay then. So should I go back to my room?"

"Yes, if you can walk. If you can't we have a wheelchair that you can use or borrow for a few days. Do you need it?"

"Nope, I think I will be fine on that matter. I can walk fairly well now."

"Good, good." Said the doctor, as he looked at his watch.

"Wow! Look at the time! It is nine o clock already! You really better be getting to your room. Patients aren't supposed to be walking the corridors after nine, so hurry."

"Okay, doctor." Said Steve, as he started walking out of the door. He shut it behind him, and noticed that he could not remember where his room is. He opened the door once again, and poked his head through. "Where is my room?"

"Well, just down the corridor, and make a left, and it should be at the end, there."

"Okay, thank you!"

"You are most welcome."

Steve set out a second time. He followed the doctor's exact instructions, and got to his room. He laid down, into his bed, and slipped away into sleep. It felt like his pillow was getting softer every minute, and he drifted off to sleep in an instant.


# Chapter 24

Steve woke up again, and looked around the room. He was still in the hospital, so it was not a dream.

"Steve, I have some bad news." Said the doctor, who was sitting next to Steve on his left, this time, but still managing to escape his view.

"What is it?"

"Well, I ran another test while you were sleeping, and I have found that you have been contaminated with the curse of an Enderman. Have you been near any exploding Endermen?"

"Yes, I seem to remember it now. I was with that chap who came in, what was his name? Old Peculier! That's it. And I was running away from a pair, maybe a trio, I don't know, of Endermen who were planning to blow the whole place up. We ran, but me and Old Peculier got engulfed by a large shockwave, and that is probably why you just found me, laying there."

"I see, so, maybe then you got hit by the exploding Enderman. Did you see any parts of the Enderman flying your way?"

"Yes, I saw the Ender pearl flying just overhead, but I didn't stay to see what happened after that."

"Ooh, the Ender pearl, that is the most radioactive part. How far do you think it was away from you?"

"Oh, I don't know, about, two, three meters?"

"Really not good then."

"Why? What is going to happen to me?"

"Well, you will turn into half of an Enderman. The only strange thing is, if you are next to an Ender pearl for about five or six, or even up to twenty seconds, it will not affect you. But you are already starting to mutate. Have you done anything else that could cause this?"

"I don't know, there was one time when I spoke the language of Herobrine, just one word, to see what it meant, but that wouldn't do anything, right?"

The doctor's jaw dropped wide open. A look of plain fright moved across his face.

"How could you… didn't you… oh my lord, didn't you know?" asked the doctor, his voice and body trembling.

"Know what?"

"That those words will corrupt you! Oh no… oh no… I am sorry, but we can't… we just can't let you stay around here. Wait, maybe you could finish your quest before you are fully mutated? No… your quest is too big to have you be done so soon. But maybe…" The doctor got up and started pacing the room, talking to half himself, and half Steve.

"I shall continue my quest, I am feeling much better. How long do I have to live?"

"I don't know, about, maybe, a week? Ten days? Maybe fifteen? I don't know… I really don't… oh no…"

"Then I shall try my hardest. What are the symptoms?"

"Well, your blood turns black, and then you can fly, then you get taller, and then… oh no… and then your skin turns black, and then your eyes turn completely purple, and then you feel an absolute, forcibly obey able, urge to serve Herobrine, and then he takes your mind, and then whatever is left of you dies!"

"So, what I have is not very good, but I must continue my quest. How long until the mutations start?"

"Well, about… *gulp* six to twelve hours."

"I must hurry then."

"Just use the window! Please, stay away!"

"Um, okay then…" Steve opened the window, and swung onto a tree. He quickly climbed off the tree, and was at ground level. There was grass underneath his feet, and there was a cobblestone path leading up to a large gate. He followed the path, occasionally hurting his feet on some pebbles, because he did not have any shoes. He was out of the hospital grounds, and he needed shoes, so he looked around for a general vendor. He saw the alchemy place, the café, the tavern, and finally, the trader. He set foot in the direction of the trader.

"We have the finest items in all of Yerta! You can't beat them! They will provide better, and last longer than ANY other item you have ever had! And for very modest prices! This iron sword? Only 14.99 gort!" shouted the vendor, as he held up various items, and he had a pile of clutter at his feet. Steve walked up to the vendor, and stopped a few feet away from the frantic mess of various items he had made, or bought.

"Hello, customer! How are you doing today?" asked the vendor, with a fake, salesman – type of grin on his face.

"Well, I would like to buy some shoes, as quick as possible please." Replied Steve, as he put his bare foot over to his left, to stop a bright red apple from rolling away.

"Well yes! I have many types. Do you like felt boots? I like felt boots. If you don't like felt boots, I have some iron boots, and some leather ones as well. Do you like it? My selection is very wide, so feel free to look around!" replied the vendor, as he said it extremely quickly. He started to abandon his large pile of merchandise, and walked into the shop. He moved his hand around in the air, pointing at different departments, and sections of departments.

"I would like some leather boots, please. I find felt too easy to wear down, and iron too expensive and tough." Replied Steve, as he looked at the colors. There was only orange, though.

"I see, like leather? Ever been cow hunting? I once went cow hunting, but the darned, cursed thing kicked me in the back. I had to go and stay in the hospital for about four to five weeks, which would convert to a month or so. My back was in agonizing pain, and wouldn't you like some premium leather instead of plain old, standard leather?"

"Well, not really. I am happy with what I have. How much does it cost, anyway?"

"The plain, rubbish ones you have are about ten gort, I'd say. Yes, ten gort. And the premium, better ones, are closer to only seventy gort. See? Not so bad?"

"SEVENTY GORT? Who has that sort of money? The king?"

"Well, he has come by here before. He bought the premium leather ones about five years ago, and does not have to buy new ones yet. Good deal, yes?"

"Are you lying to me?"

"Well, no. But, no. Just a bit of, you know, exaggeration…"

"The king did not come here, did he?"

"No, I suppose not."

"And you were only trying to get me to pay seventy gort, were you not?"

"Yes, I was. Now, to be honest, premium is only a double layer, and it has a bit of a gloss on it. Happy? Now if you tell anyone, you will ruin by business. So don't, please."

"I won't tell anyone, if you give me the boots for free."

"Premium for free?"

"No, standard."

"Oh. Okay, then." Sighed the vendor, as he slumped over to his supply crate, picked out a pair of dirty leather shoes, and handed the to Steve. "Two standard shoes. No tricks, just pure, honest leather."

"Good, now, find a better way to make money, and don't try to trick people, or I won't be happy, and I will tell people."

"Okay, just don't let out the word."

"Okay. I hope we understand each other."

"We do, sir. We definitely do."

"Good." After Steve made this conversation, he swiftly stormed away, and pushed the door open, only for it to swing back, and hit him. He stumbled back for a moment, dropped his shoes, and found himself laying diagonally against a store shelf. He tried to maintain his mood by grabbing his boots and trying it a second time, but he knew that it would not work.

After that, he was outside again. He noticed that a lot of people had probably stolen the pile of items that the vendor was showing off, considering the pile had disappeared, and there were a lot of people walking off with pockets a bit more full than they had started off with. Steve did not stop to argue the injustice of the situation, but instead started to look around for Old Peculier, who had seemed to have gone to see someone else.

"Old Peculier?" called Steve. It wasn't so loud that everybody could hear him, it was just loud enough, that you might *just* be able to hear.

"Old Peculier... that name rings a bell..." replied somebody, who had a slightly Indian accent.

"Really? Have you met him? Do you know where he is?"

"Well, I am one of his friends, when he was the mayor of the late Minsoon city. He told me that his friend, um, can't remember the name, would come out of the hospital, just over there in a few days, but he didn't know how long."

"I see. So, where did he go after that?"

"Well, he said he wanted a lay down, so he went in that direction." The person pointed towards a multistory, wooden house. "Probably the inn, in that case. I think he wants to rent a room in the inn, so that he can sleep, or lay down. He must be tired, because he has done a lot of running around and things like that. Basically, search the inn and see if he is there."

"Okay, thank you for telling me. Here, have a gort." Steve handed a dull, grey sliver of metal over to him. "Sorry, it is a bit dirty."

"Thank you very much, strange man!"

"Your welcome." As Steve said the last sentence, he started walking toward the inn, and he also noticed there were quite a few people around him, who also wanted to get into the inn, as if the king was in there. The whole crowd was shouting, chatting, laughing, sobbing, everything you could imagine, someone in there was doing it. Steve needed to push his way into the middle, so that he could slip in. He pushed past a few people, and realized they were not excited about the inn, they were all trying to beat an Enderman to death. Steve felt a wave of pity briefly for the Enderman, even though he was almost killed by them, multiple times, and he caught the curse of the Enderman. As soon as he remembered that, the pity completely went out of him, and he passed the pity of as a sign of the disease working it's way into him.

Steve continued to push passed the yelling, angry crowd, and managed to clamber up a short flight of steps, and opened the door.

"Hello! All are welcome here! Come in, come in." welcomed the innkeeper, as he put down a paper on the people who were in each room. Steve walked into the door, and saw a short, stout man. He had a greasy (or sweaty) apron on, an underneath he wore a green shirt. He had a fairly long, maroon mustache, and there was an iron mug beside him. He came out from behind a wooden counter in a dim room, with a musky smell. "How are you today?"

"Well, I am fine. How about you? Are you the innkeeper here?"

"Yes, that I am. I am the finest innkeeper in all of Minecraftia. There is not a single innkeeper finer than I."

"Good, so, I am sorry for keeping away from conversation, I have no time to spare. My question is urgent as well."

"Go on then, what is your question?"

"Is a fellow by the name of 'Old Peculier' staying at your inn?"

"Well, I don't know. I shall check my papers, and they will give me the required information."

"Good, but please hurry. My mission is in much urgency."

"Mission? Are you an adventurer, then?"

"Oh, yes. I am Steve, and I need to go and defeat Herobrine. I know it is a big and dangerous task, but it gets worse. I have captured a terminal illness, and it will make me depart from the world of the living in up to twenty days. I am going to guess about seventeen, maybe eighteen."

"Oh no, terrible. Ah! Yes! Old Peculier, room forty one. I shall ring the bell." The innkeeper reached up to a panel of buttons, and pressed one of them. Steve heard a nice, relaxing chime in the distance, and there was a voice. The voice told him to report to the innkeeper, for he has a visitor. Steve thought it sounded like he was a prisoner. In a few seconds, Old Peculier came walking out of the corridors, and looked at Steve.

"Oh, Steve, you are out of the hospital."

"Yes, I am."

"So, everything is fine, no head trauma, no blood clots or internal bleeding, yes?"

"Well, no, I have a terminal illness that could kill me in about two to three weeks, but other than that, I am fine."

"Oh, so you are not all fine."

"Depends on how you look at it."

"I suppose you are right. We better get started on the quest, then, if you are going to die in three weeks."

"I agree. Let's go, if we want to get this quest done." Steve walked out of the inn, and the crowd of people, like the pile of merchandise, had disappeared.

"Here is my pay for sleeping in today." Said Old Peculier, as he handed the innkeeper a few gort. Old Peculier then walked outside with Steve.

"So then, did you find out what happened to Skylord Lysander?" asked Steve, as he looked at the castle in the distance, that appeared to be undergoing a rebuild.

"No, but I think he blew up. However, I have heard that Skylords can be resurrected by other Skylords, and there were more Skylords on their way, so, you can never really tell. Maybe he is alive, maybe not."

"We can only hope he is."

"Yes."

"Anyway, I have decided I will use an old English sort of accent when I am near people, so that they have no idea it is me."

"Yes, I think that is a very good strategy, and it will definitely help to keep our identities down. So then, let's go. Don't want to be caught behind, while you die, or rot or explode or what ever. Are we going to try to take over another castle?"

"Um, yes, that would be great. We need to hurry though. Do you know if there is a stable in Yerta?"

"I don' kn-"

"What, what is it?"

"Steve, tell me, since when has Yerta been in the Nether?"

"What are you talking about?"

"Look! Over there, you can see netherack, and Nether castles, and the one that Skylord Lysander blew up, all of it. How is it in the Nether now?"

"I don't know... we should ask someone."

"I... can explain... to you in... your jail... cell!" rasped a voice above them. Steve bolted his head up, and saw an Enderman, floating above him. Old Peculier also looked up, and felt his heart sink to his feet.

"Not on my watch!" shouted Steve, as he took Old Peculier's sword from the holder, and pinned the Enderman to the wall by it's upper chest.

"You... fight with the... skill... of an... Enderman!" gasped the Enderman, in a surprised tone, well, as much of a surprised tone as and Enderman could manage.

"I picked up your curse, and I will die soon. You better tell me why the Nether has appeared in our dimension, or you will be killed, and my sword will slice right through your precious Ender pearl!"

"No! Not the pearl! Anything... but my... heart!"

"Then speak! NOW!" shouted Steve, as he slowly inched his sword closer to it's Ender pearl, in the chest. It was pulsing wildly now, like it was scared.

"Okay... it is because... Herobrine... and the others... used a particle transporter between... the... places... but... it went wrong! So... wrong... and it collided both realms... together..."

"That is half of what I want to know, now tell me how to reverse it? I do NOT want this place to have horrible netherack and Ghasts attack it every three seconds, because if there is no way to reverse it, then I will kill each and every one of you."

"I do not... know... ask Herobrine! He... knows..."

"Liar!" shouted Steve as he kept his sword about a centimeter away from the Ender pearl. The Ender pearl was getting very agitated.

"Okay! Okay... just... kill... ... ... I don't know!"

"Don't know what?"

"I do not... know how... to close... it!"

"Yes you do! You are just not admitting it, are you?"

" I do... not."

At this, Steve tapped the Ender pearl with his sword, or, more specifically, Old Peculier's sword, and the Enderman let out a deafening screech, that sounded like a knife against a chalkboard.

"Yes, yes I know! I... am... sorry... you just... kill... Hero... Hero... Herobr-" before the Enderman could finish the obvious word, it just fell apart, into raw pieces of obsidian. Even the Ender pearl had fallen out, and had turned into obsidian. Steve hit the loose parts of obsidian with his sword, but to no avail.

"So, basically, we have to kill Herobrine, was that what he was trying to say?" asked Old Peculier, who had been helping somebody pick up a basket of apples that had dropped to the ground in shock.

"Um, yes. I think so. He said the 'Herobr' bit, but I think I can infer from that."

"Yeah, but, Herobrine is a god! How are we supposed to kill a darned god?"

"I don't know. If we have enough of an army, maybe."

"I agree. Wait a minute, if we could get to the mainframe in which the Endermen are controlled by, we could hotwire it and turn them in our favor! That could help."

"Yes, it may help, but we can not control the Ender Dragons. They are self sentient, and they don't need a ruler to control them. By default, they will serve Herobrine. What about them?"

"I don't know, but maybe the Endermen could kill the Ender Dragons?"

"No, the Endermen are still semi sentient. They would not kill a fellow Ender creature."

"Yes, that is a slight hindrance. It could still definitely help, though."

"Also, what about the fact that Herobrine would be at the mainframe that controls the Endermen that WE want to be at? It would still end up requiring us to kill a god, you know."

"Yeah, you are right on that one. Maybe that is not such a good idea. I think we should actually just do it the old fashioned way."

"Yeah... best way."

"So let's get going, and go to another castle!" After Old Peculier had said this, he started walking in the direction of the Nether area. Steve followed close behind, and began to consider the size, and weight of the mission he was operating.

# Chapter 25

Steve and Old Peculier had just passed the wreckage of the last castle they went to, that was almost completely rebuilt with cobblestone and wood, and they got to the boundary of the luscious, green grass. Steve paused for a moment before stepping over it, just to savor the moment of being in that place, and then he stepped onto the netherack.

"Now I am out in the place where enemies are going to enjoy killing me, ripping me apart, eating me, hanging me up on the wall as a trophy..." grumbled Old Peculier, very down heartedly, and pessimistically.

"Well, it isn't that bad, you still have a sword, and you still have good skills with it, yes? It is not like you have nothing, and know nothing, and are just stranded here without a thing to eat, is it?"

"We don't have anything to eat!"

"You would be wrong in that statement, sir. For I bought twelve apples, and lots of cooked pork before we set foot!" replied Steve, as he practiced out his old English accent.

"Nice accent, and also, really? Awesome! I was just starting to get hungry now, anyway, so in about half an hour, I might have some pork."

"What about the nice, healthy apples?"

"The apples will stay good for longer, while the pork will rot quicker."

"I brought a small refridgerator."

"Seriously?"

"Yes. Only problem is, it is really heavy."

"It is a small refrigerator, of course it is heavy! Anyway, what is it powered by?"

"Red stone torches, provide everlasting power."

"Good, good. Thank you for planning ahead. Where did you get the money for all of this stuff, anyway?"

"Well, I... borrowed the money... you know, from someone..."

"That sounds pretty suspicious, if you ask me."

"Well, no..."

"You stole the money, didn't you?"

"Kind of, but, I said it was for a good cause..."

"But it wasn't this one, was it?"

"Well, depends, we *might* save starving wolves."

"That is complete dishonesty!"

"No, not exactly, it *is* for a good cause."

"Maybe so, but it is not exactly the cause they donated to."

"FINE, I will donate some of the land I conquer to a wolf farm. Why do you have to have so much moral?"

"Well, you can't really have too little moral, it is quite a good thing to have."

"But, really, you can bend the rules *sometimes*. Just not always."

"I think the rules are there to make sure you do not bend them, or to keep people safe, and not give their hard earned money to a dishonest person."

"Yeah, but, if everyone always obeys the rules completely, no body would be happy, right?"

"No, I have never disobeyed rules and I am perfectly content with my life."

"Yeah but… you are… but… you… shut up."

"You can't really win an argument with me!"

"I said shut up! I have the food, now if you bug me too much, I could just eat it all and give you none!"

"You wouldn't really do that to me, would you?"

"I said 'shut UP!'"

"Okay, I will."

After that, they walked a long way in silence.

"You do know I did not really mean that I would starve you, right?"

"Well, duh. You are not really the type of person who would starve somebody because they have a different opinion."

"I was only joking. In fact, that does seem really mean. Like, Adolf Hitler sort of mean."

"How?"

"Well you know the Jewish people, they just had a different idea of what happens to the order of the world."

"I suppose you are right, but personally I do not believe somebody as evil as that even existed. I think it was just a false story from the people in the mixed lands."

"What are the mixed lands?"

"They are the places where the spheres exist. That is where the people who call themselves 'humans' and where our language got founded. I think that it is just a story."

"I am from the mixed lands, and Hitler is definitely not a myth. He existed all right."

"What did he do?"

"I will not go into it in any detail… he did horrible things to the poor innocent Jewish people."

"Ah, I see. I will not ask any more about that."

"So, where exactly are we going again?" asked Steve.

"Oh, um, I think we are going to one of the other Nether castles, but I could be wrong, so do not take my word for it."

"I am assuming that we were not going anywhere extremely important,"

"Not important!? What are you talking about?"

"I do not mean like, not important I mean, more like, we do not need to go their exactly now, and if we walk or run will not make a life or death decision."

"Yes, I thought that would be what you meant, but I wanted to make sure, to make sure that you did not mean that our mission to break Notch free from Herobrine, and to obliterate all evil from the very essence of Minecraftia."

"Wow, and oh, yeah. That is what I meant. Otherwise, that would not really be good if I did mean that. I would probably get kicked off the journey by you, if I said this whole mission was not important."

"I might not kick you off the whole trip, but I certainly would talk to you in a slightly angry manner, because this trip is extremely dangerous, and even more so important, considering we are determining the fate of Minecraftia and what not, so, yeah. You would probably still be on the mission though, because I need all the help I can get, and if you are off the trail, I can't very well do that, can I?"

"Yes, you have a point there."

"Well obviously I do, because if I did not have a point, then I would not have mentioned that in this particular conversation. It is like saying 'I think 'so and so' should be the president of the United States. And the person you are talking to says something like 'I like donuts, but I really like the ones with the thick icing, and the custard inside.' It just would not have any continuity. Using the color of your own shoes in an argument about who has the most kills. Pointless. Anyway, just because I say that I will probably not kick you out of what we have of a team, does not mean under any circumstances that you can behave like an idiot, and eat fireballs, and be a jerk. Eventually I will just draw the line, and leave without you, so do not act like an a- I mean jerk."

"Well yes, I am not going to be obnoxious because I will not get a punishment, I am in fact older than about ten, nine, or even eight and a half. I *am* 41, maybe 42 years now, and I am not a hyper brat who disobeys orders. I went and killed a load of Endermen, and now I think I am completely justified in being able to be treated like a 41 or 42 year old."

"You do not remember your own age? Why?"

"Well, I was born in the mixed lands, and I do not know how much time passes there to one amount of time that passes here, or even if they are the same. In the mixed lands, my birthday would be in about a month or so."

"Hm, I see, you would be about 47, maybe 46 by now. Everybody assumes you are dead."

"Oh, lovely and cheery."

"Not to rain on your happy thoughts and parade there, but why is your arm laced with black veins?"

"Well, that would be the disease I have."

"What disease was that? I could not quite catch it."

"Well, it was the curse of the Enderman, nasty. It will turn my veins and blood black, then it will do something else, maybe it will make my eyes go purple or something, then Herobrine will try to corrupt my mind and I will want to go with him, and then my skin will go black, then the thoughts of the Enderman inside me will take over my brain, and eventually I will die. Good news, it will take a while, and the stronger the mind you have, the longer it will be put off."

"Where did you find that out?"

"The doctor at the hospital told me from underneath his own sobbing mess in the corner of the room, and then he told me to jump out of the window."

"Well, strong reaction. Anyway, I was not talking about that, I was talking about the fact that 'the stronger brain you have, the longer the symptoms will be put off" seemed to come out of nowhere."

"Oh, that one? I made it up to keep you from dropping your stuff and running away in fright of my disease."

"Why would I do that?"

"Oh, I do not know, it might be very contagious, for all I know, so just do not think about my disease, and then you will not be scared about catching it."

"Is it contagious?"

"Well, the doctor cowered in the corner when he read it, so... bler mur hur hur." Steve trailed off at the end of his sentence.

"Hey, you did not answer my question, you just, kind of trailed off."

"Well, it might be a bit contagious, just as long as we do not cut open our veins and press them to each other, I hope it will be fine!"

"You are basing this on nothing what so ever, are you not?"

"Yes, but it is nicer to think about in this way."

"But it is not the truth."

"Oh whatever..."

Suddenly, Steve cringed over in pain, grasping his arm.

"Um, Steve?" asked Old Peculier, as he walked over to try to catch Steve before he fell over and hurt himself on the netherack on the ground.

Steve just continued to cringe in pain, grasping his arm still. The arm he was grasping was the one that the black veins had almost conquered. After about fifteen seconds, he had stopped twitching and what not, and he seemed to be out of his pain very suddenly.

"I think that was the curse of the Enderman, working it's way through the pain receptors in my veins." Said Steve, as he got up from the ground, rubbing his arm, to make sure that it did not get caused by a very tense muscle or something of the sort.

"Yes, I do believe so. Looks quite nasty, that curse. Is there any cure?"

"Well, I have heard that for some people, if you kill another Enderman it goes away."

"Maybe, I do not know. I thought you killed that one, back in Yerta, and you still are not better."

"No, that one exploded for some reason, I do not know why, but it exploded in the middle of the sentence."

"Oh yeah. Maybe we should kill another one, and hope that that cure would help the disease."

"Maybe if I killed Herobrine that would cure it, because if Herobrine is like the leader of all things evil and what not, then if you kill him, some process happens and it may turn me back to normal!"

"I think that is the most possible solution. But first, we have to complete our mission."

"I agree. We must proceed with maximum haste, sir!" replied Steve, one again practicing his old English, sort of like a knight-ish accent.

"Well we do not really need it, here. We are already at the castle, so we presumably just bust down the doors and go berserk on everything that is alive."

"Yep, basically the plan."

"Good idea. What are we waiting for?"

"Well, we are about to attack one of the main bases of Herobrines, so, I think I need about thirty seconds to cope with the fact we shall be utterly and completely obliterated."

"Well, pessimistic, but fair enough." Steve and Old Peculier stood outside the castle for about thirty seconds, as they had said, and then they started to walk to the door. Steve stupidly knocked on the door, and then hit himself in the forehead in frustration.

"Who… i… is… i-it?" rasped a very hoarse voice, presumably that of an Enderman.

"It is your destruction!" shouted Steve, in a bad attempt to patch up the mistake of knocking on the castle doors,

"What?" rasped the Enderman, who sounded very confused.

"Well, first of all," said Old Peculier, in his 'oh yeah I am a brave knight' sort of voice. "We are your absolute bane, your complete undoing, and your worst fear. We are what keep every single one of Herobrines creations awake at night. You can not deny our existence, or escape our skills, because it is your time to be killed, and you can not do anything about it."

"Yes... we... c-can."

"What can you do?" asked Steve in a more fearful then anything sort of voice.

"Kill... y-you."

"Oh, well that is what you will fail at, because we are experts at the whole fighting thing."

"Stop bragging, Steve. It only makes it worse."

"Sorry."

Suddenly, they heard a loud roar coming from inside the castle, and then a much larger gate next to them appeared. It opened up, and let out a large black dragon, with purple eyes. Steve and Old Peculier knew what it was instantly when they heard the roar. It was an Ender Dragon.

"Ender Dragon, um, Old Peculier, what do we do now? Do we run, or do we fight it and die, or so we run and die, or do we kill ourselves and die?"

"I would just say fight it and die, and maybe we will not die. Maybe we can kill it, and then we will be very happy, as well as shortening down Herobrines supply of tame Ender Dragons, won't it?"

"But what if we die?"

"Then we die fighting for a good cause; one better than starving wolves."

"Yes, You are right there. We do not really have much of a choice anymore, actually, because it has caught eye of us, and there is a rider to control it. Think about it, the skill of a fighter mixed in with the pure awesomeness and power of an Ender Dragon. Basically, it means that we are pretty close to person mush, and that would be very bad, obviously."

"Well, brace yourself, because the Ender Dragon is coming to eat us, or maim us, or brutally harm us in some nasty way." As Old Peculier said this, the Ender Dragon came swooping down towards them. Steve could see it's lips twitch in anticipation of burning them, or in anticipation of snatching them up with it's teeth and eating them.

"HORU'U THROF MOK LAIA!" shouted the Ender Dragon, and as he said it, he seemed to speed up in his rocketing descent towards them.

"Duck!" shouted Old Peculier, as he flopped over onto his stomach, and then he rolled over onto his back so that he could see the Ender Dragon, just in case it landed and was going to claw them to death. Steve jumped down as well, and just in time, too. The Ender Dragon swooped right over them, letting out another deafening roar. The Ender Dragon seemed to check whether or not it had caught Steve and Old Peculier, by feeling at it's mouth, and looking around at the claws, and then started to check itself for any sign of damage, such as one of them sticking a sword up into the air, and hurting the Ender Dragon. It looked around it's chest and legs for a moment, and then it turned back to face Steve and Old Peculier, and started to fly towards them again. I seemed to know, or to learn what they had just done, and instead of just swooping merely feet above them, as it flew closer and closer to the ground, it started lowering it's tail to drag along the ground, that caused a path of destruction and wreckage in it's path.

"Look out! The Ender Dragon is coming to us! Again! We need to either stand up to it and try to kill it, or we just run!" shouted Steve, as he pulled his sword out of it's holster, and stared at the oncoming tail.

"I say we need to fight it. Try running behind its tail, and we might be able to kill the rider by running up the body and killing him from behind, and then we could much more easily kill the Ender Dragon, because it would have much less strategic abilities!" shouted Old Peculier in reply, as he started to climb a rock, so that he might be able to jump onto it's face or something.

"I definitely agree, yes, listen, if you can distract it, I can run around to the back!"

"Already on it!"

The Ender Dragon had caught sight of Old Peculier, and was charging at him at a very alarming speed. Old Peculier was getting very worried about the Ender Dragon, and if he could not jump on to it's face correctly, then it would just eat him, and that would be the end of that. As Old Peculier became more a more worried about these things, he decided, to get a better chance of survival, he would jump. The Ender Dragon was about ten or eleven meters away now, and it would be at Old Peculier in about two, three, or maybe even one second. Old Peculier was not happy. When the Dragon was about two meters away, he made the most important jump of his life, and landed on the Ender Dragons nose. The Ender Dragon roared wildly.

"Your uncivilized standards are no match for my fighting skills!" shouted Old Peculier, as he tried to impersonate Steve doing his old English, sort of medieval accent.

The Ender Dragon just roared again, and started tossing its head back and forth.

"Old Peculier! I made it on top of the Ender Dragon!" shouted Steve, from the saddle on which the rider originally was sitting on.

"Good! Now can you come up to me, and pull me over there, please? The Ender Dragon is trying to shake me off!" shouted Old Peculier in reply, and he reached out his hand for Steve to hold, and pull him off the head of the Ender Dragon.

"I will, but then he will just try to shake us off down here, maybe instead of you coming to me, I will come to you!" shouted Steve, as he started to move closer to Old Peculier.

"Great idea! Then we can kill it by repeatedly stabbing it's head or something!"

"Well, yes, I suppose that would work!"

Steve pulled himself up to the head of the Ender Dragon, and started using his sword to dig into it, and pull himself up, as if he was mountain climbing.

"Be careful, Steve! If you keep this up, then you will not be able to come up here, because the Ender Dragon will realize you are not the rider and start attacking you with it's claws, so just watch out!" shouted Old Peculier, as he drew his sword, and started hitting the Ender Dragon in an attempt to either distract it, or just to kill it, like their plan had suggested.

"I will be more careful! I am almost there, not long to go!" replied Steve, as he pull himself up onto the Ender Dragon by pulling on Old Peculier's arm. He took his sword, brought it above his head, and mercilessly brought it down harshly upon the Ender Dragon's head. The Ender Dragon let out a giant roar, and then it started to swerve down, into a large bed of sharp rocks.

"What are we going to do? If those rocks touch us at that velocity, then we will be sliced to pieces, and we will not be able to complete our mission!" shouted Old Peculier, as he moved away from the now limp head of the Ender Dragon as it fell out of the sky.

"Well, I suppose that we could just go to the body, and hope that the rocks are not too tall, or too sharp, or too smooth."

"Good idea, just help me get to the torso, quickly!" shouted Old Peculier, as he scrambled down to the other end of the Ender Dragon's body.

"Okay!" shouted Steve, as he was already at the safest part of the torso, and he was pulling Old Peculier's arms, to help him to get to the safest part with him. The Ender Dragon was falling perilously fast, and it was not good at all. It seemed to tilt it's wings in the direction of the wind, as if to decrease the drag to get down to the bottom of the sharp rocks made of netherack.

"Hurry, Old Peculier!"

"I am almost there, stop panicking! STOP PANICKING!" shouted Old Peculier, as he was panicking more than Steve, actually.

"We only have about five more seconds of air time, come on! Let's go!"

Soon, Old Peculier made a last jump, and landed on the thickest area of the torso, with Steve. Suddenly, the Ender Dragon stopped, and they knew what had happened. At first, they did not know whether to be happy or sad about it, because of the shock and drama of what had happened before. They noticed sharp, broken pieces of netherack showing through various parts of the Ender Dragon, and in some places, there were very large amounts of netherack showing, but then there were also very small bits of netherack showing, no larger than your thumb, and no thinner than paper.

"We survived! Yes! We survived!" shouted Steve, as he slowly and cautiously climbed off of the Ender Dragon, and walked around the field of shards. His expression was slightly lagged, though, because he only started to feel happiness about three seconds after he realized what had happened.

"We did survive! And we killed the Ender Dragon, and we captured another one of Herobrine's castles!"

"How come? I thought we still had to deal with the army of Herobrine's that is still in the castle, do we not?"

"No, I saw the people there run away from the sight, when we started to win the fight."

"Brilliant! Really, brilliant! But it definitely goes to show how hard it is to kill one of those, let alone tame one, and keep it happy once you have tamed it!"

"I agree. So, anyway, should we go inside the castle and start up the thing that makes Notch's people with the army and what not come down from there?"

"I suppose we should, that would be the best way, in my opinion. If we do not do that, then Herobrine's forces will just easily walk over to the castle we just had, take over, and leave. Simple, but if we actually claim it, instead of have it as 'Oh Notch will find it eventually' attitude, yes, I think we should go and claim it, basically."

Steve and Old Peculier just left the scene of the Ender Dragon, and walked inside of the castle, to find that it looked identical to the one they had taken over last time. They just took this as meaning they could follow the same steps to bringing them, and that would be fine.

"So, last time, all we had to do was walk down this corridor for ages, and when we come to the end, we just replace the little black crystal there, with the black crystal we have in our pockets, and then it should be fine!" exclaimed Steve, as he stuck his hand into his pocket, and pulled out a small black crystal, made of obsidian.

"Yes, I think that is what we did last time. Sounds quite simple, doesn't it, a bit too simple…" muttered Old Peculier, as he trailed off.

"I do not think so, I just think that it really is that easy. Would Skylord Lysander really lie to us? I think not. Let us go and do it, and if it does not work, then we will look for a manual of some sort."

"How do you know there will even be a manual in this place?"

"Well, Skylord Lysander said that there is one on certain matters in every single place."

"But if Skylord Lysander is wrong about the first thing, what makes you so sure that he will definitely be correct about the second thing?"

"I am not saying he will definitely be correct, I am just saying that he probably will be correct."

"Based on what?"

"Well, he has never been wrong before, has he?"

"But just because you whack a pig and it does not attack you, does not mean it will never happen to you, does it?"

"Well no, but that is a completely different sort of thing. Taking advice, versus hitting a pig, a bit different. Besides, it can hurt any body, can it?"

"No, it can not hurt any body, but it might waste our precious time."

"Listen, I will try it, but if I am correct and it does work, then I will have to say the following: 'I told you so.'. Now if you have any problem with that, then I will have to say 'I told you so.' Because I know you will have a problem with it. Problem?"

"There really is no way out of this, is there?"

"Well, no. Not really, unless you are right, in which case I will not say it."

"Hey, it sounds fair to me."

"Actually we are about to find out anyway because we are only a few feet from the room, if you look ahead of you." As Steve said this, he pointed to the room with a small pool of water in it, with a little stand for a crystal.

"Prepare to be proven!" exclaimed Steve, as he skipped ahead, pulled out the old crystal, and inserted the new one gently. Suddenly, the water started to have ripples appear in it, and there were some materializing bodies in it. "I am sorry I have to say this, but I told you so! I definitely told you so! I told you Skylord Lysander was correct, but nope, you did not believe me for a second, but look! They are materializing right before my eyes, using the method Skylord Lysander told me to use! And to think you would do something as silly as to question me and Skylord Lysander, no, we were right all along!"

"I never agreed to you rubbing it into my face, did I?"

"Well, no, I suppose not, sorry Old Peculier."

"It is okay, but really now, we need to hurry. Let us go out of this place, and find another castle, or something like that."

"Good idea."

As Old Peculier and Steve ran off down the corridors, the people continued to After they had already run off too far, and were leaving the castle, not only were normal people from Notch's lands beginning to form, but also someone that had been killed –twice- was materializing. It was Markus Persson, who was being sent down from Notch's lands to take care of the castle. He was sent back into the physical world, once again. Markus looked at his hands as they began to form. They looked more like mundane stubs at the moment, as it was too blurry for him to see any formation of hands, let alone fingers or any other intricate feature on that level. Soon, Markus could feel himself breathing, and he could just about see his feet begin to form outwards from his legs. After a minute or two, he stepped out of the small pool, and was fully formed. He looked around at the walls of netherack, and looked back at the other people who were behind him, still in the materialization pool. He was wearing some shiny chainmail armor, and he had a sword in a holster at his belt. He started to walk through the other rooms, and decided that he should remodel the place, perhaps make it out of cobblestone, or something else that is not netherack. He took out a large, iron pickaxe from his backpack, and started to mine a little opening in the netherack, full of stone, as a material for his remodeling of the place.

# Chapter 26

Steve and Old Peculier were waking towards the next castle, when Steve started looking at his arm. The blood contained in his arm was completely blackened by his disease.

"Wow, my arm is, well, really blackened now." Exclaimed Steve, as he checked his arm over very thoroughly.

"Yes, well, of course it is. What about your other arm, has it made any progress there?"

"Well, yes, a little bit. But not much really. It has not gotten past my elbow yet, but I do not think it will be long before it surges ahead, like it has on my other arm."

"Yes, I very much agree."

"We do have to keep going, and we do have to hurry up, because if we do not hurry up, then I will die before we have a chance to complete the mission."

"Yes, you have said that about a hundred and fifty three point one five times."

"What do you mean, 'point one five'?"

"Well, you probably got distracted in a few of them when you were point one five through the sentence."

"A few of 'them'?"

"A few times you wanted to say it."

"By the way, did you actually count the way?"

"Yes, I was bored."

"From what?"

Instead of replying, Old Peculier just stared at Steve for a few seconds, and then looked ahead again.

"How could I bore you?"

"One hundred fifty three point one five times, Steve. That is a lot of times!"

"Oh, yeah. I suppose that is a bit annoying. I once had to sit next to a really annoying child on the bus. He kept asking me 'Where are you going?' and I kept replying 'I am going to school, little child.' And eventually after a ton of repeats, it turned into him asking 'Where are you going?' like normal, and then I said 'Listen, I am going to ki- I mean, I am going to school, and if you still do not know, I advise you to d- I mean go ask some other person, you blood sucking demon from the deepest and darkest pits of hell, who has been personally been sent up from the horrid fires down there from Satan, to make my life a misery in five minutes. The thing I did not realize is that the little boy's six foot tall father was standing behind me, and he basically bashed my head in when I got out of the bus."

"How old were you when that happened?"

"Well, I was going to college, so that would mean, maybe about thirty one, thirty two, thirty nine, something like that."

"I see. Why could you not have just fought back or something like that, and you would not have been hurt quite so badly. And also, why could you not just explain the situation to the parent, right?"

"Well, he did not really give me the chance to do any explaining, and I did not fight back because he was about six and a half feet tall, and very strong. If I did fight back, then I would not be here today, probably, because he would have just killed me and left me somewhere or something like that."

"That is not very good, obviously. Did you not just try to run away from him? Or did you report him to the police?"

"Well, I *did* try to run away from him, but he was just so fast. I tried and tried to run, but I just could not go fast enough, and he grabbed the scruff of my neck, and pulled me back, and punched me in the stomach. I did report him to the police, and I think he is still in jail for the moment, but it will not be long until his sentence is up and he can just walk out of the jail, and continue to do that to people. Apparently it is his third time in jail now, and the child was not really his, it was the child of another person and he was just a psychopath or something."

"Why did he do that to you?"

"I did just say I do not know, but after I got home, I went to the hospital for internal bleeding in my left arm! Not good."

"Where are all the people around here, I can only see netherack, for miles around!"

"Wait a minute, what about the terraforming, we can still see that happening, because it is starting as we speak, right now!"

Old Peculier and Steve stopped in their tracks, turned 180 degrees around on their heel, and watched the netherack being turned into grass, trees, stone, all of it, just like had happened last time they had captured a castle, the same castle that Skylord Lysander had been blown up inside by the Endermen, and Skylord Jasper.

"Wow, looks quite nice,"

"Yes, I agree, just a little less land that Herobrine controls, and that Notch does control."

"Two castles down, eight, is it? To go."

"I think it is ten castles that we have to destroy, and we got two of them down, so yes, I think so. Eight castles to go down. But the problem is, the more we destroy, the more well prepared all the others will be."

"What do you mean?"

"Well, first of all, they would notice that all their castles are being obliterated by us, and more importantly, all the reinforcements and supplies that would be sent to the other castles, would instead be sent to the remaining castles, so therefore they would get more advanced and more prepared then the last one, until we get to the last castle, which will be extremely well prepared, and will be the equivalent of fighting all the castles at once."

"Good point, but what do you expect us to do about it?"

"No, nothing really, I was just saying that was a hindrance, and it could be very annoying and get in the way of our ideal plan."

"Well, perhaps so, but it does not mean that our mission is going to be impossible, does it?"

"No, for the last time, no."

Suddenly, they noticed tracks for a mine cart going along the ground. Steve walked over to the tracks, and very carefully observed where they headed to. They went through a large netherack wall on one side, and through a wall on the other side, as well. They could here a faint rumbling sound, and it got louder and louder by the second. Steve looked further down the track, and saw a mine cart was rocketing along the tracks, with a storage chest in it. There was no person in the actual mine cart, instead there was only the lone storage chest, bobbing about slightly when it came over a dent in the tracks.

"We need to stop the mine cart now." Said Steve, as he placed a large rock in front of the path of the mine cart. The mine cart very quickly struck it with a loud 'bang' and it slowed down a lot. It rolled gently a few meters away from where it had hit the rock, and eventually stopped altogether.

"Okay, so now that it has stopped, we can search it for supplies." Replied Old Peculier, as he peered over through the tunnel to see the mine cart.

"That is why I wanted to stop it, so that we could do precisely that."

"Oh, yes, that would make the most sense, what are we waiting for, anyway? Let's go and loot the supply chest!"

Steve and Old Peculier quickly walked up to the supply chest, and opened it. What they found was incredible. They did not know whether to be happy or sad as to them finding out the Herobrine could make it, but they had it. They had found obsidian, but not only the obsidian, there was obsidian armor, obsidian sword, obsidian tools, even obsidian jewelry. They each took a set of obsidian armor, and they also each took an obsidian sword. They were surprisingly light, but only in comparison to a sword, or to an iron sword. They slipped on the armor, and the armor *moved* around them. It molded itself to fit their exact body type, and everything. The armor seemed to be hugging them with cold, unforgiving tendrils. At first, the armor seemed cold and heavy, but once it started moving, it got very warm, and very light. It fit them both like a second skin.

"Wow, is this armor *actually* moving around our bodies? Or am I just hallucinating?"

"I think it might be… is there a gas leak around here or something else that would cause two people to have extreme hallucinations?"

"Not that I can see, why would there be gas around here, anyway?"

"I do not know, but also why would this armor be alive or liquid, or at least possessed of some type."

"There are many questions, so I just say forget them all, and just go with the flow. It works, do not question it or we may lose it, do not think about it too hard, just go with it."

"I agree, that is probably the best method. So, do you think this armor is very tough? Looks and feels pretty tough."

"Let me scratch it, and see what happens."

Steve scratched the armor with his sword, and it definitely did leave a mark. There was a large, white stress line across the breastplate.

"Well, good job, Steve. You managed to destroy a bit of your armor."

"Yes, but how else could I find out if it was hard or not? This is practically butter soft."

Suddenly, a purple glow erupted from the white stress line, and the obsidian repaired itself.

"Oh, wow, um, why did that just happen?"

"Well, from what I have gathered, obsidian holds very special and possibly magical properties, and it just healed itself."

"Now that is what I call durable outer casing!" joked Steve, as he held his hand up in the air, expecting a high five.

"No. Just, no. Not until you can pry open my cold dead hands."

"Oh really?"

"Wait! I have and idea, if obsidian does have special properties, then you should not be hurt at all if I whack you with my sword!"

"Um, Old Peculier, let's not get too trusting into the obsidian, it is still just a material, you know!" exclaimed Steve, as he tried to back away, but Old Peculier had already drew his sword, and swung a blow at Steve. "OW!"

"Oh, sorry!" apologized Old Peculier, as he inspected the damage that had been done to the armor. Surprisingly, the damage line was exactly as deep as the stress line that Steve had made. It repaired itself quickly.

"The armor might not be broken, but the blunt damage to it still really, really hurts!" scolded Steve, as he stood up, after being knocked over from the force of the blow.

"I said sorry, but I learnt something very important about this armor. Do you want to know what it is?"

"Well, obviously I do! What is it?"

"I think that it has an adminium layer sandwiched between two layers of obsidian."

"And what is adminium?"

"Well, some people call it bedrock, and some people call it the end of the world. It is the substance that is at the very bottom of the Over world, and the Nether, and in the Nether it is at the very top. There is no adminium in the End, however, there is void that will kill you after a certain time of exposure, because it is breaking the laws of physics to go there. It is the void, where no types of matter can ever exist, so it will just rip you apart quickly, and cleanly."

"Not nice stuff, then?"

"No, adminium is not very nice. The only way that they could be making these sorts of things are if they are creating another part of the Over world, and using the newly generated bedrock to generate inside the two layers of obsidian. This really is not good."

"Why do they need to do all this just to get some bedrock?"

"Well, bedrock is unbreakable, and the only way they can get it to be placed somewhere, is by artificially generating it."

"But why is that so bad?"

"Well, you know why the Nether is in the same place as the Over world?"

"Not really, could you tell me?"

"Well, yes. It is there so that it will teleport to the Over world, and then all they have to do is put down an obsidian sandwich in the correct place, and the adminium just automatically generates inside! It works, so they will do that for a very long time until the Nether becomes too unstable, and disintegrates. Adminium or bed rock, is what protects the different realms from the void that would normally just rip everything apart."

"Oh, okay. Can I keep my armor?"

"Yes, yes. You can definitely keep it. Even though it has been made from the bed rock that is highly unstable, it has already been made, and we do not want Herobrine getting his hands back on this sort of thing."

"Good. I like my armor."

"So do I."

Suddenly, Steve and Old Peculier heard a loud thump come from the mouth of the small tunnel they were in. It was a repetitive, bouncing noise, and when it bounced, they could hear the singe of something burning.

"What is that out there?" whispered Steve to Old Peculier, in fear that it would find out that they were hiding in there.

"I do not know. But judging by the bounce rhythm, I would say some sort of slime."

"But what about the burning sound that is coming from the so called 'slime'?"

"Well, it could just be a fire slime."

"Does that even exist?"

"How should I know that? I am surprised I know as much as I do about the matters."

Suddenly, the slime appeared around the corner of the cave, and it was, in fact, slime. It was black and red, with orange eyes, and had a sort of a spring underneath the main body. It looked directly at Steve and Old Peculier, and started bouncing towards them.

"Old Peculier, I think that it just found us, and now it is going to burn us." Whispered Steve, as he got up, and pulled Old Peculier's arm, to force him to his feet.

"Then let's run away from it!"

"But we *could* kill it, because that would be fairly useful."

"Useful how?"

"Well, we could harvest interesting materials from it, could we not?"

"I suppose so; okay. I will help you kill it."

Steve ran up to the large, fiery slime ball and stuck his obsidian sword into it. The end of the sword opened up inside the slime and spun around about fifty times a second, and then it retracted and pulled out of the slime. The slime's springing method of transportation ceased, and then it split into two smaller ones.

Steve hit the slimes once again, but they just split into more of the smaller ones. The smaller ones were green though, and they did not make any attempt to attack Steve or Old Peculier, and instead just idled around aimlessly.

"I think that should do it." Said Steve, as he kicked away a few hyper slimes that were buzzing around his feet.

"I agree. That was actually fairly easy to do, with this new sword. The sword seemed to guild itself through the air. It was like the sword was holding and moving my hand, instead of my hand moving and guiding the sword. I felt very strange."

"It felt the same way for me, it just kept keeping control over my hand, and it seemed to do as I wished, without me actually having to move any part of me."

Steve looked at his new sword very carefully, and ran his fingers down the sharp, serrated edge of it.

"Steve, do you think that Herobrine's forces already have this sort of amazing supplies?" asked Old Peculier, as he tucked his sword into the holster.

"I would probably say so. It is not going to be pretty when we have to kill some sort of enemy with this standard of armor. Not pretty at all."

"That is very, very bad. The last things we want is for Herobrine to have this super armor, and super sword, because he could just put his troops into it, and then the troops are almost invincible, because they have a bed rock layering in their armor. We would only be able to get to them through the eyes, the mouth when they are talking, and the nose. And not even all of Herobrine's army even have a nose or mouth!"

"Well, we should get going any how. We need to get to the third castle of Herobrine's, because we obviously really need new land."

"Wait, first, I think we need to find out if Skylord Lysander really is dead."

"Really? I think that Skylord Lysander is definitely dead. I mean, he did just explode."

"Even so, but he could still be alive somewhere."

"Okay, maybe he could be alive. Should we check the land of the Skylords?"

"Yes, that would help. If he is anywhere, he would probably be there. Now, where can we get back to the Over world?"

"I do not know, we need to find a portal."

"Well, yes, I know that."

"Maybe there is a spare portal we could use in the castle where Skylord Lysander exploded, maybe."

"Yes, I agree. I say that there probably is a fair chance, because last time we went there, I could see the portal there, but Jasper would not let us in."

"Do you not mean *Skylord* Jasper?"

"No, remember? He had his Skylord license invalidated by Skylord Lysander, and that is why he blew up Skylord Lysander."

"Oh yeah, that was why he died... oh yeah... I think I must have forgotten."

"Well, you did just under go some fairly serious amnesia, you know."

"Okay, so it is not *all* my fault that I actually forgot the death of our friend, Skylord Lysander."

"Anyway, should we chance to go back to the castle? Even though there might be more homicidal Endermen with a Skylord?"

"I think that the odds of that happening twice by the same person are highly unlikely, I mean, who would want to do that *again*, after they already got executed?"

"Well, yes, I do not *really* think it would happen again, but there is always the possibility. If they got there once, I bet that the Endermen could very easily get there again."

"It is a chance we have to take. If we want Skylord Lysander back, we will need to get to him, via the closest, or easiest, or maybe even only route back to the Over world."

"Wait! I have an idea." Exclaimed Old Peculier, as his entire face lit up.

"Well, don't just stand there looking smug, what is it?"

"I have heard about an Elemental Lord centre, where all the Elemental lords are allowed in, and they can all share training, or resources."

"Good idea, we can go there, search for Skylord Lysander, and maybe get some Waterlords to join us."

"Why do you think only Waterlords will want to join us?"

"Well, I thought that Skylord Lysander said that all the Earthlords and all the Firelords were dead."

"But their training is not, so we could still get people who have the training that the Earthlords and Firelords used to join us, and it will be as good as an actual Firelord or Earthlord."

"I see, well, I think we should just go there, and have a look to find who we can find."

"Sounds good to me."

"By the way, which way is that castle?" asked Steve, as he looked around, and peered through caves and tunnels of netherack.

"From my reasoning, I say that way, but I could be wrong. I just know that I see  large castle that looks like the one that got blown up, because it is made out of cobblestone, and it has the same layout of grass and stone just outside."

"Yes, seems like your reasoning is correct, in that case."

"It is not so much reasoning, as good eyesight and memory."

"Whether it is reasoning or good eyesight and memory, we need to go to the castle."

Then let's go! For the last time before I start leaving without you, because you just seem to want to stand here and talk for the next million years about it."

Steve and Old Peculier said nothing beyond that; instead they just started walking towards the castle.

# Chapter 27

After about two hours of walking in complete and utter silence, they arrived at the castle.

"Well, here we are, let's just hope that no body inside the castle wants to kill us, maim us, or to do any other bad thing to us." Mentioned Old Peculier, breaking the awkward silence.

"I think it is unlikely, Old Peculier." Replied Steve, as he knocked on the heavy and slightly rusty metal. Someone on the other side answered the knock.

"Hello? It is Steve and Old Peculier, we would like to come in, please."

"Steve and Old Peculier! Nice to see you again. Come in!" replied some person, who sounded exactly like Jasper.

"Jasper? What are you doing here again?"

"Have no fear, Steve. I am on probation. I have a couple of *very* nice guards with me, who will barely let me do anything!" spat Jasper, through clenched teeth.

"Calm it down now, Jasper. If you are not nice, then you will not have any more probation for another month."

"Yes, Gurthan."

"Not Gurthan, the name is 'guard' to you. Repeat after me: I am sorry *guard*, but I have used your private title."

"I am sorry guard, I have used your private title." Droned Jasper, right after a very large sigh of frustration.

"Better."

"Anyway, won't you come in, let me just undo the latch, and I will tend to your needs."

Jasper slowly slid the small bronze sliver of metal through the loop, and then the door opened widely.

"Hello, Jasper. What news is there of Skylord Lysander?"

"Well, I think he is okay, he did not get hurt too badly, but I did. I permanently broke my left index finger, and I also absorbed a terminal amount of dangerous radiation. I am not feeling very well right now, either."

"Good, now, could we use the portal to get back to the Over world? We need to find Skylord Lysander, because we need help in our mission."

"Yes, your mission, to kill Herobrine or something like that, right?"

"That is the one."

"I have something for you, but it appears you have already found it."

"Found what?"

"Well, found the obsidian armor? You know, the stuff you are wearing?"

"Oh yeah, we found it in a mine cart, that we managed to stop using a giant boulder. It put up a very large jolt, but the stone could handle it. The cart spun off the track, and so we went and saw what was inside, and we saw this armor just sitting there, inside of the cart. We took it, along with these lovely obsidian swords."

"Well, I found these in a mine cart track, that runs about a quarter of a mile away from my actual house, and one day the track stopped working while the was a cart near my house, and so I decided to loot it, and I found all the lovely armor. It was quite lucky, really, because I needed this armor, and I was planning on buying it from He- I mean, um, nevermind."

"So, why did you need it?"

"I needed it because, of, um, Herobrine was sending troops to attack where I was, and, um, there were lots of enemies, troops, loads! Um..."

"You are making this up, no?"

"Yes, I am. Sorry."

"What is the real reason?"

"Well, it was way back when I was working with Herobrine, and I robbed them so that I could use them to make sure I did not die when I tried to capture you. Sorry."

"Well, at least you were honest about it. We need to hurry, because if we do not hurry, then we will not have any time to be able to continue our mission. As it is, I have a very, very painful disease that is eating away at my soul as we speak, and I have about thirteen days to go, now."

"What disease is it?"

"It is fatal, now shut up, I mean stop talking, and let us through. We really, really need to hurry up, because if we do not hurry up, then we will have no time to actually do this. Hurry!"

Steve looked around desperately for any sign of the portal.

He saw in the distance, a very large obsidian frame, containing a lighter purple jelly. The jelly was moving about, as if it had newts in it, just like the last portal they had encountered. Old Peculier and Steve both remembered the feeling when they entered the portal, and how the jelly seemed to slide down their back, very slowly and uncomfortably. They could remember how cold the jelly was, and how what seemed to be newts slowly crawled, very slowly around their backs, and eventually there were so many slithering beings, that it felt like their whole body was engulfed in these wriggling creatures.

The only difference from the one they were seeing before them and the one that they had remembered, is that the one they were seeing was very agitated. The skin of the actual portal inside the obsidian frame, was very agitated and was actually bending away from the frame, and what looked like the large newts inside, were running about as if they were flaming, and ate a lot of sugar.

"The portal is this way, then." Said Jasper, as he walked into the room with the agitated portal.

"What is wrong with it? Why does it look so... disturbed or hyper active?" asked Steve, as he took a very careful look at the portal.

"Well, it just means that the portal is a bit old, and has gone out of 'tune'."

"What do you mean, 'out of tune'?"

"Basically it means that the portal needs to be reignited, some new obsidian, basically get a new portal, or extremely refurbish the current one. You would need to brush all the dust off the thing, poor some water or another lubricant over the sides, where the obsidian frame meets the portal itself, you know, the whole works for it."

"Well, will it harm us if we go through it as it is?"

"Let's just say it should not cause too much harm, if any. It might stick you at another place in the Nether, because it might not still be in sync with the one it is supposed to be linked to."

"How bad can it hurt us, at maximum?"

"I would say, in a nutshell, basically,"

"Get on with it!" shouted Old Peculier, who was getting very tired of this game of guesses, and him not really having a good explanation for anything that they ask him.

"Okay, okay. I would say that it would cause anything from a bit of pain in one of your limbs, maybe a graze or two, to minor mutilation, perhaps of a finger, or of a toe, or something small like that, or maybe even some sensory damage, and it might make you blind, give you a cataract, completely blind you, or make you deaf, almost deaf, you get the picture. But it will not kill you, even in the state it is in, and ooh, also, it might cause a bit of mutation."

"What sort of mutation?"

"Well, mutation, it might turn you half chicken, or maybe what happened to that poor pig like fellow down there might happen to you, but I would say it is unlikely. It could give you a tongue on your forehead, an ear on your chest, anything like that. It was a bit like a teleport, in a book I read, where the teleportation device, and in our case, it is a portal, anyway, the teleportation device made one of the smartest men alive – into a human yo-yo! How is that for poor designing! But Notch designed this one, and Herobrine merely moved in, so it should not hurt you too much, bottom line."

"I see. Is it worth the risk, do you think?" asked Old Peculier, as he looked at Steve, then the portal, and then imagined him as having arms for legs and legs for arms. In his head, he then put some taste buds on Steve's head, and put and ear on his chest, like Jasper had said. He smiled to himself at this thought.

"Well, actually the chance of a risk is really quite small, so I would not worry about it. I would go through it, and I think there is only about a twenty percent, or maybe a ten percent chance of actually getting hurt in it. It is fairly safe, just not as safe as a normal portal would be."

"Good, I think that we should just go through it, and get it over with. Do you agree with me, Old Peculier?" asked Steve.

"Hmm, yes, I think so. We only have a limited time, and maybe, if you get mutated, it would mutate out your disease? I do not quite know how it works."

"True, but unlikely. Let's go then, I am voting for the positive."

"Me too, positive all the way."

"Then, let me just dust it, just to make sure that it is completely, well, I say completely, I mean, almost completely, well, almost, at least. You should have nothing to worry about."

"Then hurry up, please. We really are very limited in our time. We need to go!"

"Okay, okay. I will just blow it, and brush it off, because apparently I do not have time to actually get a rag or something..."

"Yes, that would be appreciated. I think that would definitely be appreciated. We do not *really* need a rag to dust things, just use your hands, and you can wipe it off after if you want. By the way, quick question, quick answer please, where is the rest of the team?"

"Oh, er, scavenging mission for supplies."

"Thnak you. Tell them they need wool on their next mission to place rags closer to the portal, next time."

"Well, I already did, but they are rubbish at shearing sheep. Anyway, here is your portal! Hop in, and hope for the best of luck!" said Jasper, as he took his hand away, and gestured for Steve and Old Peculier to enter the portal. They did as they were gestured to do, and as they wanted, and the stepped into the thick jelly. The newts seemed to instantly notice this, and they started to slip and slither around Steve and Old Peculier, and the outside world seemed to face, and become more purple, and eventually the nets started slithering over their eyes, as well, but for some reason, it felt, *right*, like it was actually normal. They found this very weird, and then seemed to wake up from a doze when they got to the destination. It was, in fact, where they wanted it to be, and they quickly realized, *those were newts crawling around me, and onto my face and everything!*, and then eventually, they checked themselves for any sure signs of harm, or mutilation, and Steve checked his arm, to see if the disease had gone, but it was still there, and his vision was slightly tinted purple, just a little, tiny bit.

"Steve, I just noticed. *Those were NEWTS!* Oh my, not good, not good, but it felt like it was fine, until I realized actually what was going on. I do not have any signs of brutal mutilation, I feel fine, I am not missing a finger, still got all my teeth, I am fine. How about you?" asked Old Peculier, as he ran his finger down each of his teeth.

"Nope, I think I am fine as well. But my disease did not mutate away, I still have it. So, are we at the centre of the Elemental Lords?" asked Steve, as he looked around for a sign, to tell him.

"Well, not to my knowledge, however, judging by that sign, just over there, I will say that the centre of the Elemental Lords is right over there, about fifteen, twenty, twenty two or so meters away from us right here."

"What made you choose twenty two? Sounds very precise."

"Oh, well, I was just guessing, I just though that it was a bit less than twenty five, so I just chose twenty two."

"I see. So, just over there, is it?" asked Steve, as he pointed to a large sign, advertising it.

"Yes, I think so. It does say: Centre of the Elemental Lords – Here. Visitors welcome. Empty spaces: fifty three."

"Fifty three empty spaces! Wow, must be a very boring, or unpopular place."

"No, that is for visitors, and the maximum capacity is around two thousand, maybe two thousand and five hundred people there. It must be fairly packed."

"Two thousand and five hundred people! It obviously is VERY popular, and VERY interesting."

"Well, not so much interesting, as that people want to meet the Elemental lords, and apparently, it says right next to the sign, that they have actually used the ancient runes and artifacts from the time of the Earthlords and Firelords, and they have retrained a group, and restarted the clan!"

"Awesome! Maybe we can get a good amount of companions, to help us kill Herobrine. That would be best in my opinion."

"I agree. Let's hurry! We have a bit of a problem with just standing away from it and talking, don't we? We seem to do that almost every time we see something." said Old Peculier, as he started walking towards the main gates.

"Yeah, we need to stop that, and actually go places." replied Steve, as he followed Old Peculier to the main gates. The main gates were very large, with spikes at the bottom, and there was a guard, who had a lever, that presumably shut the gates. The gates were on a rail, inside a sort of downwards – curved stick, or tree, closer, and the gates were just slotted in, but it looked like an incredibly sturdy arrangement, when in principle, it sounds quite flimsy. They walked up to the security guard, and asked if they could go in.

"Hey, excuse me, guard, but are we allowed into the Centre of Elemental Lords?" asked Steve, very lightly.

"Well, depends." replied the security guard, who had a surprisingly gruff and rough voice for his appearance, of being fairly short, and quite large. He was wearing a very large, blue hat, that blocked out most of his face, except for his mustache. He walked up to them, and continued his talk. "Do you think you are allowed in?"

"Well, yes, I think so." Replied Steve, as he looked at the person. The guard seemed to be looking at Steve's feet, because it looked like that was the only thing that he *could* see underneath his hat.

"Then, I will have to ask you why you want to."

"Because, well, we are on a mission, and we want to destroy Herobrine, to free Notch, and to claim all the land in Minecraftia to be his. We have gained a fairly strong foothold for Notch, but we need to get a better one, by gathering Skylords, Waterlords, Firelords, and Earthlords to help us in this mammoth task."

"Well, seems legit. I will let you in. But if I catch you two causing any trouble, then you are going straight to the slammer, understand?"

"Yes, we understand, guard, sir."

"Good. Go on then."

Steve and Old Peculier entered the site, and looked around.

"So, first of all, we need to find an advertisement area or a barrel to rant from." said Steve, as he looked around for a place to advertise their need.

"A barrel?" chuckled Old Peculier, as he started looking around as well.

"Well, those guys are standing on barrels, ranting for things. That one is doing an out right crazy person style rant, with a capital r, capital a, capital n, and a capital t. And all the letters are really, really hairy, big and fat, for his 'insane prices that will make you go insane because you will catch its INSANITY!' He is a bread salesman. He is trying to make everyone in the whole place buy bread, I think that we are allowed to pick up a barrel and start shouting at people from it."

"Okay, but I really hope you are right. *sigh*. Okay, there is a barrel right over there, you can go and pick it up, stand on it, and do a nice, long rant." Sighed Old Peculier, as he dug his face into the palm of his hands, and kept his face there for a few moments. Steve actually walked over to the empty, disused barrel, passing; many others that Steve had failed to notice. He picked up the barrel, and noticed it was in a very poor state of disrepair. It looked almost rotten through completely, and the wood was growing a lot of mould on it, and hosting a variety of different bugs. He picked it up anyway, and put it down closer to a large crowd, and stood onto it. He started his rant.

"Come, one and all! To listen to my important matter! Come on! I have a very important point to make, and it involves pay, if you get involved!" shouted Steve, and this gathered a very large crowd of people. They were standing there, hoping to hear a rant about something good.

"Now listen! All of you! Listen! I need help for a vital mission! I need lots of Skylords, Waterlords, Firelords, and Earthlords! Come on, who *is* an Elemental Lord, anyway?" asked Steve, and about half the people there put their hand up.

"Good! See? Now I bet you want to hear about what my mission is, do you not? Because my mission is VITAL! My mission is to kill Herobrine, and to free Notch of his torture and slavery, by always trying to delete him from Minecraftia, but it never works, Do we want to end this misery?" asked Steve, and the crowd actually shouted back.

"YES!" shouted the crowd.

"And who will join me, in destroying the very forces of evil?"

"WE WILL!" shouted the crowd, once again.

"Then let's go!" shouted Steve, as he go down from the barrel, and started forming a line in front of him. "Neat line, please! I need a line to assign you all very important orders, choose to obey them if you are not too much of a pansy for the mission!"

At an instant, the crowd developed a very long line in front of Steve, and assigned them each orders. He assigned some of the orders to go and take the castles in the Nether, and some of them are to join him, in his final journey, to the End. Only very few got picked to join him, and most got picked for other jobs, such as go out and rally up against the legendary King Ender. After about fifteen minutes, everybody had a mission.

"Now go, and complete your task! I hope you can, but together, we will destroy all evil related to Herobrine! There shall be no casualties taken if we all work together!" Steve shouted this, very loudly to the crowd, and the crowd just cheered. Eventually, they all left to complete their task, except for the four people who were instructed to stay with him.

"Now, as for you four, each of you are and Elemental Lord, and all different. You will come with me and that person over there, named Old Peculier, he has been very helpful to me, and I am sure that you can be just as helpful. Now, first, my name is Steve, and we should now introduce ourselves, in counter clockwise direction."

"Okay, my name is Waterlord Katrina." said Waterlord Katrina, as he looked at the next person in the row.

"My name is Firelord Jonathan." said Firelord Jonathan.

"My name is Earthlord Tsuna." said Earthlord Tsuna.

"And my name is Skylord Gordon." said Skylord Gordon.

"Good, now that we all know each others names, I should tell you something about me. Basically, I have a terminal disease, and it will kill me in about twelve, eleven days, now. I need your help, because I can not just kill a god on my own, I need to have, what is a little bit less than an army to kill Herobrine. It will not be easy, but I think that I can do it with the help of you four."

"Good, I think I am fairly confident on what to do. I am good with my blade, and I can utilize any fire that might occur." Said Firelord Jonathan.

"Yes, brilliant. We need all the help we can get. Now, is anyone here, not officially an Elemental Lord?"

"I am official." Said Earthlord Tsuna.

"Me too." Said Skylord Gordon.

"I am also official, I have a sword to prove it!" said Waterlord Katrina.

"Ditto." Said Firelord Jonathan.

"Good, we do not want any mix ups about whether or not some body is an Elemental Lord or not, because that could be a criminal offence, I think, impersonating an Elemental Lord. So, are we all ready?"

"Well, yes, I think so." Replied Firelord Jonathan. "Just one question, what *exactly* is our plan?"

"Basically, I think that Earthlord Tsuna has a stronghold, somewhere, because most Earthlords do, or so I have heard." Replied Steve.

"Yes, I do have a stronghold. It is about a half hour, maybe fifteen minute walk that way."

"Good. We will use the End portal to get us into the End, where we will attempt to kill Herobrine."

"I do have a portal, but, well, it is not functioning." noted Earthlord Tsuna.

"What? Why?" asked Skylord Gordon.

"I do not have enough eyes of ender to open the portal."

"Why can you not just open it anyway?" asked Steve.

"Actually, we need the eyes of ender so that the high intensity tau-neutrino beam will concentrate itself through the lenses, and make a controlled rift in space-time, that could lead us into another brane of reality." Said Waterlord Katrina, who was very knowledgeable about the subject.

"How do you know all this?" asked Steve.

"I researched this sort of thing, before I could become a Waterlord."

"Oh, yes, because Waterlords can make all sorts of technology. They are the scientists of the Elemental Lords. Anyway, does anyone have any eyes of ender?" asked Steve.

At that point, Old Peculier walked over to the crowd. "Well, I have... 1... 2... 3... 4... 6... I have 8 eyes of ender, is that enough?" asked Old Peculier, as he counted small beads, with narrow slits in them.

"Yes, I believe so. I do think that that should be enough eyes of ender." Said Earthlord Tsuna, as she started looking in the general direction of her stronghold. "Oh, and, by the way, it is old, and giant, man eating silver fish have colonized the place."

"Brilliant." said Skylord Gordon, in a tone that was dripping with sarcasm.

Earthlord Tsuna lead the group to her stronghold, and it took a total of exactly twenty minutes to get to the stronghold.

The stronghold was made out of stone bricks, and there was some moss growing around the walls. The stronghold did not look very nice at all. It was a dug out hole in the ground, with a corridor branching off of it.

"Is this it?" asked Steve.

"Yes, I believe it is. Unless I have lead you to a place that looks identical to mine, and it is in exactly the same place as mine, then yes, it is mine." Replied Earthlord Tsuna.

The group walked through the little dirt hole, through the entrance, and they were in a dimly lit hole.

"Lovely. Really, looks... lovely." Said Old Peculier, as he jumped away from a wall, where he could hear some rustling.

"You don't need to be sarcastic about it, I know it is dirty, and not very well kept at all, but don't sugar coat your answers, or make them sarcastic. Through the corridor, and there will be a frame for the portal." Said Earthlord Tsuna, as she started walking through the corridor. The corridor was fairly short, and it lead to a much brighter room, with a blue and black frame, lying horizontally. It had a pool of lava underneath, and made an eerie hum.

"Okay, so, presumably this is the portal?" asked Old Peculier.

"Yes. Put the eyes of ender into the sockets, on the frame. Ii will activate the portal, and let us go through it. Do not touch the ones that are already on it, just add."

"Okay. Let's go." Replied Old Peculier, as he carefully placed eyes of ender onto the frame, and listened as the hum got stronger and louder. When he put the final one in, there was a burst of energy that knocked him back a few steps, but it did not hurt him too much. He peered down, into the portal. It was very different from the portal to the Nether, considering it had a black portal, with little pin pricks of light emerging from it, and this portal had more *depth*. It seemed to be that they could see into the realm they are about to go into.

"I will go first." Said Firelord Jonathan, who was the most experienced fighter there. He walked up to the portal, and jumped in. he completely disappeared, without a trace when he entered it. There was no more than a small ripple in the surface, that evened out quickly.

"Do you want to go first?" asked Waterlord Katrina, as she looked at Earthlord Tsuna.

"Me? Well, maybe, okay. The order from now on, to preserve time, is: Me, Waterlord Katrina, Old Peculier, Steve, and then Skylord Gordon." Replied Earthlord Tsuna, as she walked up to the portal, and slowly hopped off, and into the portal. She disappeared, just like Firelord Jonathan had done. Shortly after, Waterlord Katrina jumped into the portal, and then the rest jumped in almost at the same time.

End of Part 4

Part 5
The End

# Chapter 28

Steve felt a painful tingling in his arms, and it was spreading to his legs, and upper torso. He felt that it was so painful, as soon as he materialized into the End, he dropped on his knees, and then dropped lower even more so, and was writhing in pain, flat on the ground.

"Steve, are you alright?" asked Old Peculier, as he noticed that this was really the worst time for him to be suffering from his disease.

"Yes... I think so-o-o-o!" exclaimed Steve, as another burst of pain appeared in his head.

"Steve, maybe you should sit here. Go back through the..." said Old Peculier, but he stopped when he realized that the portal the had jumped through disappeared. "... portal."

"What is wrong?" asked Steve, struggling even to say those three words.

"The portal is gone!" exclaimed Old Peculier. It had vanished. They had just entered the End, and for the portal to be gone, was not a good sign at all. Steve saw a figure riding an Ender Dragon charge towards them.

"Old Peculier! Look out!" shouted Steve, but it was too late. The Ender Dragon was mere meters away from Old Peculier, and it swiped in up, in one snap of it's jaws. Old Peculier took out his small dagger, and tried to stab it before it could throw him into it's mouth, but it was no use. The person riding swiftly brought his hand down on the back of the Ender Dragon, and the dagger flew out of Old Peculier's hand. It landed on the End stone with a loud clatter, and an Enderman broke it in half. The Ender Dragon quickly snapped up it's head, and gulped down Old Peculier, as if he was a potato chip. All Steve could do was lay there in pain, and watch while he got eaten.

"Too late!" snapped a harsh voice, coming from the person on the back of the Ender Dragon. "He is dead! And so will you be, you small, insignificant worm!"

With that, the person dove down to where Steve was, and jumped off of the Ender Dragon.

"Ender Dragon, finish off his little friends." Said the person. The Ender Dragon made a little snarl, and then flew off in the direction to where they were fighting. "And now, as for you, I would like to finish you off personally."

"Who a-a-re you?" asked Steve, in as much of a fearless voice as he could manage.

"I am the one you made an arrogant attempt to stop. I am Herobrine. But why would I tell you? I will tell you. Because if I told you who I was, then you would know, in your tortured afterlife, what a failure you are. And how you endured all that pain and suffering for a stupid and pointless cause."

"Perhaps, but what about if I *do* kill you?"

"And what if a snowball in proverbial hell comes to life, pukes out a top hat and starts dancing?"

"Your words mean nothing to me. Let us just get this over with." As Steve said this, he drew a fairly long sword, and charged into Herobrine. Herobrine easily dodged, and clenched his bare hand into a fist, that caused immense pain throughout his body.

"Stupid man, you should never have come here! Then again, if you hadn't, I would not have been able to have so much fun with you!" snapped Herobrine, as he suddenly released his grip, and Steve fell down. He hit his lower jaw, and dropped his sword. Steve attempted to open his mouth and shout in pain, but his jaw would not move, so all that he could manage was a mundane groan.

"Ohhhh…" mumbled Steve, through a mix of pain, and more pain.

"I should have known that this fun was short lasted. I am in a nice mood – I will kill you now." Said Herobrine, as he drew a rusty, dirty sword from a holster. "But wait! I have a better idea! Instead of killing you now, I will freeze your muscles, and kill your friends, but make you watch!"

"Boe…hoe't vo at!" said Steve again, in a failed attempt to say 'No, don't do that'.

"Oh, yes!" shouted Herobrine, as he picked up Steve and made all the muscles in his body clench up, including his jaw muscles, that caused incredible pain. Steve's skin was going black incredibly quickly. In a few seconds, his whole body looked like an Enderman.

Herobrine picked off the Elemental lords, one by one, while the Ender Dragon fought them. Firelord Jonathan had already been eaten, as he was the most daring soldier there. Waterlord Katrina was severely injured, and was also the first to spot Herobrine approaching.

"Look out! An enemy coming from over there!" she shouted, but before anyone could do anything, Herobrine moved his arm swiftly, and Waterlord Katrina just fell dead.

"Herobrine! It's Herobrine!" shouted Earthlord Tsuna.

"Where?" asked Skylord Gordon, but while he turned to look, he let his guard down, and the Ender Dragon swiped him up, and carried him away.

"I will finish this!" murmured Earthlord Tsuna to herself, and charged to Herobrine. She found her limbs fall off, with no signs of blood or wound, and she just fell, or melted into smaller blobs, until there was nothing left of her.

"Now, enjoy the show?" asked Herobrine, as he turned to Steve.

"Aahh!" mumbled Steve.

"Good. Now you can play a part in it as well! Ever fancy plays? The ones with tragedies at the end? Because you are part of the tragedy. See this syringe? It contains poison! One poke with this needle with kill you. And... oops!" exclaimed Herobrine, as he prodded Steve with the needle, and it just barely broke his skin. "You are dead, aw, so sad."

Suddenly, Steve got a smug smile on his face.

"What is so funny?"

"Ahind oo!"

Herobrine turned around, and he saw a sword coming down on his head very quickly. Before Herobrine could do anything about it, it had lodged in his head, and he fell to the floor.

"Steve!" shouted the bearer of the sword, who was Markus.

"Arhuh!" exclaimed Steve, with his jaw aching, and he was getting extremely tired from the poison.

"Are you okay? What did he do to you?"

"Oihun, ma arm!"

"Oyster?"

"Oihun!"

"Poison?"

"Eh! Eh!"

"Oh no, Steve!"

Steve suddenly died, and fell to the ground. What Markus realized is that he would have died even if he wasn't poisoned, because the End was slowly disintegrating. Large portions of the End were disappearing, and then, the part Markus and Steve were on, started to disintegrate. It didn't hurt at all, but for Markus, the whole world, what he remembered, predicts, and what he sees all went white for him, before he finally stopped thinking altogether.

The End…

**… maybe**

978-1-4716-1721-8
ISBN

By Alex Caswell who is the only, sole creator.

Published by Lulu.com

This is the original version published in 2012.

The book is published in 2012.